Witch Way Home

ROBERT WRIGHT

Shylah
Have a great
...

DEDICATION

For Scott who showed me how to set my imagination free
and Sherrie who keeps me anchored.

CONTENTS

ACKNOWLEDGMENTS

Thanks to the friends and family who encouraged
and supported this book. To my chief editor, cover artist, manager,
and favorite fan – thanks for all the hard work you did and for
putting up with the attitude I inflicted on you.

CHAPTER 1

The room was dark and dank, with moisture running down the walls in the flickering torch light. Movement from a slight, bent, hooded figure stirs the small fire under the cauldron sitting in the middle of the room. The dark, small figure slithers back and forth between an old book and the bubbling, revolting mixture cooking in the blackened pot; mumbling in an ancient, forgotten tongue of evil. Suddenly she stops and glares into the deep, dark crevices of the room. She cocks her head as though listening to a black whisper. As the liquid bubbling from the black pot hisses and boils over, she turns back and starts to stir the mixture. The small figure stops and glances over her shoulder, cocks her head again then she gives a shake and a mad cackle. "Now that little brat will be brought back home where I can deal with her!"

In the dark corner, a small laugh echoes and slowly fades away.

———————————

Slowly I wake to the feel of soft, cool breezes across my bare skin; the soft warmth of the sunlight kissing my closed eyes; the steady drone of nearby bees as in a summer meadow buzzing in my ears. Since I fell asleep last night in my small bed, huddled under my covers to fight off the cold, damp, Washington chill I must still be dreaming. Sitting up and looking around, I decide yep, I must still be dreaming as I take in the trees with their purple leaves waving in the breeze, the five foot multi-colored flowers with bees the size of small dogs flying around them. As I sit on the velvety soft red grass, that my butt is planted on, I think either I am having one weird hallucination or to quote one famous lost girl, "*I am not in Kansas anymore*".

Shifting around to check out my surroundings, I see the one constant in my life, Mr. Blue. He is my safety blanket, my constant companion since I was a little baby. A ragged, ratty, blue stuffed bear that has never left my side from the crib to now. Mr. Blue has been with me wherever I have gone; looks like he has followed me even into my imaginings. I also notice that wherever **here** is, my old warm, ratty bedtime sweats are now replaced with a simple shift seen in B movies about gladiators. The outfit is short, white, and has this strange design on the chest. It's a red circle with a straight line running horizontally through the middle of it, with two wavy lines above, and three below the middle line. Even though I don't pretend to be a clothes horse, nor follow the latest fashions, this is really beyond my standard, everyday outfit.

Well, might as well get up and see about finding out where I am. I start walking over to a small path that leads off into two directions. One way looks to wander up to some hills in the distance with what appears to be a large building perched on top of it. The building reminds me of pictures I have seen of castles in some dark fantasy tale. The other direction leads off through some black menacing woods. The dark trees growing together form a menacing, shadowy tunnel over the path that looks like the maw of a great beast ready to swallow all who wander through.

"Well Mr. Blue, what do you think? Big building on the hills, or dark, creepy looking woods? Yeah, I think so too, to the hills we go." Hey, what can I say? I'm not one of those outdoorsy types; I like my comforts. And yes, I do talk to my teddy bear. What can I say? I'm a little weird that way.

After what seems like hours in this dream, walking through this weird, but beautiful landscape it would be nice to see someone, anyone, who would tell me where I was. I feel better now that I can see I'm getting closer to the big building on the hill with each step I take. Even though as I get closer to it, the feeling of dread grows inside me, and the thought of heading back to the dark woods flutters through my mind. I can see the house on the hill looks like the wicked castle from some fairy tale. It is a dark and forbidding building, even in the daylight.

As we get closer to the hills, the landscape is changing, ascending. More rocks, boulders and small, wild groves of trees have sprung up around us. Maybe I need to stop and think this direction over some more before we go any further. Maybe that dark forest wasn't such a bad way to go.

My stomach grumbled; I looked around for food. "Look Mr. Blue, an apple tree," I said. Sort of, well, maybe, I guess. If you can call a tree that is silver with black-looking objects the size of grapefruit on them an apple tree. Well, they look like apples, if a little large. My stomach rumbles from hunger again.

"Well what do you think, buddy, should we grab a squat and try the treat?" I ask my little buddy. I picked the smallest of the fruits I could find, but found it hard to take a bite out of the strange looking black apple. Despite my rumbling stomach, I soon drifted off, lost in thought, trying to figure out what was going on in my life and when was I going to wake up.   CRUNCH! I slowly looked down at the dark fruit in my hand; it now had a big bite taken out of it.

"What the heck!" I looked at Mr. Blue who had what looked like a dark smear across his face. Now I know I must be hallucinating when my stuffed bear takes a bite of my apple. Suddenly, the smell of chocolate cake drifted up from the apple in my hand. My stomach rumbled and I thought oh well, might as well as I took a small nibble. "Yep, it's chocolate cake." This was starting to be a dream I could get into. Now I wonder how the water tastes, as I eyed a small stream flowing next to the trees I was sitting by. It looked a little muddy, but what the heck I was starting to get a thirst on. Looking into the small stream, I could see my reflection. Yep, it was still the same me, with my blonde hair and blue eyes looking back. With a small sigh, I took a sip from the stream to quench my thirst. Wow, chocolate milk! Now I was really, really starting to get into this dream.

After several more apples, and a full belly, I reluctantly decided that we should stay on the path we had headed down. Hopefully finding someone to tell me where I was. Even though this place was starting to give me the willies, I figured it was better to have a roof over our heads than stay in the open. The spooky, old building had that run down look that most evil castles in fairy tales have. Or maybe it was that I hadn't seen any movement around the place and it was starting to bother me a little more than before.

I had just taken a few steps when I heard what sounded like a thunderous herd of creatures coming around a bend in the road. Before I could move, about five strange somethings came marching around the corner, stopping as they caught sight of us. Out of all the strangeness in this dream, these were the weirdest creatures I had ever seen. They stood about four to five feet tall with huge feet, big floppy ears, and protruding bellies. They reminded me of pictures of goblins from some D & D comic I had read, down to the green skin and tusks that curved up from their bottom lips. They actually had this old armor, spears, and other fighting stuff. Whatever I had for a snack before bed last night was definitely off my list from now on.

"The Princess, grab her," yelled the biggest and meanest looking of the group.

"Yep, time to rethink those healthy bedtime snacks my foster mom has been feeding me, Mr. Blue." I stepped backwards and turned to run when, as is my usual graceful manner, I tripped over my own two feet. As I went down, I lost my hold on Mr. Blue and he flew through the air straight toward the group coming at us. I know it's not much of weapon to throw at a bunch of mad, charging green goblins, even if it was by accident.

I flailed my arms, trying to stop myself from falling, and in a flash of light and a puff of smoke, Mr. Blue was not a stuffed bear anymore. Where he had fallen now stood a great, black, fuzzy monster; eight feet tall with horns coming out of the side of his head and huge paws with razor-like claws. Mr. Blue looked like a demon from hell, complete with smoke rolling out of his wide, black nose and flaming eyes staring around.

With a roar, the demon that used to be my cuddly teddy bear slashed his head to the right, impaling two of the smaller goblins on his horns. With a shake of his head, the goblins flew into a nearby grove of trees. I could hear the bodies flying through the trees with the sound of broken branches and, probably, broken bones and skulls. With another roar and a swing of his giant paw, the other two, smaller, goblins made a large splat against some boulders by the side of the road. They formed two small, green splatters on the rocks as they slowly dripped onto the road.

"Yech! Gross."

Slowly my giant savior turned my way with a huge grin on his face. "Mr. Blue, are you in there?" I queried. With a grin that grew even bigger, if that was possible, and a wag of its small stub of a tail, it turned back to the last goblin left standing.

"Princess, there seems to be a slight misunderstanding," the goblin gasped with fright, as he started to shake and back away from Mr. Blue.

"Misunderstanding, my butt," I snapped back. "You and your buddies were trying to kidnap me, at the least and at the worst . . . I don't know what you were planning," I said, not so much scared anymore as starting to get a little peeved at this big goblin.

With that said, I heard a low rumble of anger from the big, black monster standing between us. As he took a step toward the leader of the goblins, now really trying to edge away from us, and, with a shriek, he threw his arms in the air and tried to run away. My big buddy pounced on him, quick as a flash, like a cat on a mouse, and had him hanging in the air in his big paw. With one quick flick of the paw, the goblin spun in the air, went past the biggest set of teeth this side of a T-Rex and disappeared down my, hopefully, new buddy's throat.

"Well that was certainly gross." Hoping that that short, green meal was all the demon was hungry for.

The new Mr. Blue came rambling over to me like a little puppy looking for his praise. Looking in his eyes, I could see, deep down, that this was my buddy and childhood friend. Reaching up, I gave him a quick pat on the head.

"BURP!!!!!!!!!"

"Oh that was so gross,", I gasped, trying not to upchuck. Monster breath, I thought as I was covered in a green cloud. Oh well, at least Mr. Blue looked like he felt better after that revolting explosion.

"Well, now what do we do, old buddy?" Just about then, Mr. Blue got an odd look on his face and then started to make a sound like a cat hacking up a hairball. I took a step back warily, I've seen some nasty hairballs before, and hated to see what a eight foot monster would cough up, especially after eating a goblin.

Splat! He spat out a pile in front of me. "Yeah, big guy, that was even more disgusting than being burped on by you," I told him. This was turning more and more into the weirdest dream on record, I was sure.

Glancing down at the big pile of goo, my eyes caught a shining light. It looked like a staff of some sort, a gold rod with a jade dragon circling around it. At the top of the staff, the dragon had what appeared to be a fire red jewel in its jaw.

Staring into the goopy mess on the ground, mesmerized by the shiny staff buried in the pile, I thought what the heck, not like it hasn't been gross today already. I grabbed the staff as quickly as I could, thinking that way I would get it over quick, and get less goblin/monster goo on me.

As my luck was going today, as soon as my hand touched the staff two things happened. There was a boom with the bright light of an explosion, and the sensation of flying through the air. Well, I thought as I hit the ground, and before I surrendered to the dark, I sure hope I wake up from this dream now.

CHAPTER 2

Slowly rolling over and shivering in the cool darkness, I clutched Mr. Blue in my arms. Now that was one weird dream. Goblins, chocolate cake apples, and streams of chocolate milk, I thought groggily. As I came around from my slumber, I began to notice that my butt was lying on grass, and I could hear the wind through the trees. I rolled over and slowly opened my eyes and stared at the strange stars in the sky.

"Well, shoot Mr. Blue; guess we're still here, wherever that is."

Fully awake now, I noticed a strange tingling on my right arm. "What the heck?" Looking down, I saw that there was a tattoo that looked like the staff Mr. Blue had upchucked, what seemed like hours ago. It looked like the same gold rod, down to the jade dragon entwined around it, and it even had the red jewel clutched in its jaw. Now who would put a tattoo on me when I was out, and why? Bit by bit I turned my arm around to see the whole tattoo; then slowly shook it to get rid of that darn tingling feeling.

As I shook my arm with my new tattoo, to the right a small ball of red energy flew from my finger tips and engulfed a nearby tree, causing it to burst into flames. "Oh whoa, that was so cool!" Boy, I could have used that a little earlier, I thought. "Oh well, can't moan over spilled milk, as my momma used to say."

As I looked around, I found Mr. Blue changed back to his teddy bear state, lying on the ground. I could now feel a soft thrumming coming through the ground I was lying on. It was as if drums were playing or I was feeling the vibration from lots of marching feet. It sounded almost like an army, like the one that was now pouring forth out of the castle on the hill. Those guys almost looked like the goblins that I had met earlier in the day. If five goblins were a problem, an army of goblins was not my cup of tea, I thought.

"Well Mr. Blue, I think it is time to blow this place," I squeaked, but where? Looking around, I saw what looked like a crack between two boulders at the side of the road. Slipping through the crack, looking for a place to hide, I could see a small path climbing the side of the hill. Right about then four of the goblins came down the road with what looked like a large lizard on a leash. The lizard was about six feet long from nose to tail. It was covered with fur all over its six legged body, and it had a large nose that was glued to the ground like a bloodhound on a scent. I figured that these goblins, with their pet, were probably the scouts for the goblin army and only the first of my problems coming.

"Well Mr. Blue, would be nice if you were that monster again," I sighed, looking down at my fuzzy blue teddy bear and wishing for one big, black protector.

That's when that weird little lizard let out a screech and headed to my hiding place with four goblins right behind it. Without conscious thought, I flicked my tattooed arm and watched several of those strange energy balls erupt in the middle of the group, lighting them up like Roman candles on the 4th of July, and burning the ground around them.

"Well so much for that problem, Mr. Blue." Not waiting around for any more company, and escaping from the smell of smoldering goblins and lizard, I followed the small path, hoping my improvised goblin barbeque would take care of any scent I left, in case there were any more of those six footed bloodhounds tracking me.

The path I followed led up and away from the castle and, as I climbed the walls, navigating the path's twists and turns hid me from the road below. The sun slowly rose as I climbed the path. Soon I came upon a small ledge, hidden by an old, gnarled tree that hung off the side of the cliffs. As I sat to rest, I could look down on the road I had been on and see that the first of the main body of the goblin army had reached the burned area. I held my breath as they cast about the area, looking for my scent, but soon I saw them head down the road that I had traveled on back toward the old forest. With a sigh of relief, I headed back up the path through the twists and turns I had been following before.

Soon my climb started to level out and I came upon an open area with a small waterfall that filled several small pools, and a grove of fruit trees that lay before a dark cave where I could see wisps of steam curling from deep within it. I quickly looked around for any danger, but seeing nothing I climbed down to the pool before the cave and slipped my feet into the cool water.

"You do know that your feet are in my drinking bowl, right?" a grumpy, gruff voice echoed from the cave.

"I'm sorry," I said as I gathered up Mr. Blue, and jumped behind some rocks.

"Who's there, and what are you?" I queried, peering into the cave in fright.

"Why I am me, and I am a dragon," came the answer from deep in the cave. Looking closer, I could see two large, red eyes as they stared out at me from the cave entrance. The steam that I had seen earlier now issued from between those ruby orbs.

"And who are you exactly" I asked?

"Why I am Ernie," the gruff voice answered and, as I watched, a dragon twenty feet long, and ten feet high slowly emerged from the cave. He had green scales the color of jade, with a golden belly, and ruby red eyes. His wings were folded against his body, but when he fully emerged from the cave, they spread out into two mighty spans each half his body's length. He was a magnificent and proud creature in his stature and breadth.

"Oh, now I know I have to be dreaming, first goblins now talking dragons," I mumbled under my breath.

As the dragon bent his head closer to me, he asked "Are you all right, Princess?"

First goblins, now dragons. "Why does everyone keep calling me that?"

"Calling you what, Princess?"

"That! Princess!"

"Well, that's who you are, the dragon Princess." Ernie pointed at my arm with one claw. "See, you have the mark on your arm."

"Oh I see, I guess."

"Wait a minute; if you're a dragon, and I'm a Princess does that mean you're going to eat me?" I whispered as I slowly backed up to put some space between us.

"Oh, that's just gross!" rumbled Ernie. "I am a royal dragon, I don't eat people like a common goblin and, Princess, where are your wings?" Ernie asked as he slowly eyed my back. "Have you lost them?"

"Sorry this is one Princess that wasn't born with wings," I answered as I glanced over each shoulder, just to double check.

Slowly, Ernie lowered his head to look me over. He looked at the design on my new outfit and gave a grunt. "Now I see where your wings are, Princess."

"Well I am glad you can see where my wings are!" Giving Ernie air quotes with both my hands and really starting to get tired of this whole conversation that seemed to be going in circles, even if it was with a talking dragon.

"I just mean, Princess, that your magic is being held in check by the symbol on your outfit. That's all." As he said this, Ernie traced over the strange design on the front of my outfit, sending a tingling feeling throughout my body. "I mean you probably even have trouble making a fireball, Princess, don't you?"

"I'll show you how much trouble I have, you overgrown iguana!" as I flicked a fireball at his nose.

"Very cute, Princess, that tickled." Ernie chuckled as he raised his head and unleashed a fire ball the size of a small car into the air. "Now that's a real fireball, Princess," he said with a hint of laughter in his rough voice.

"Yeah, yeah very funny, you big lizard, but how am I going to get my magic back?"

"Why, that's easy, Princess" said Ernie as his claw reached up and ripped the shift I was wearing in half and flung it into the air, where he incinerated it with a quick snort of flame from his nose.

"Yeah, well that may have solved one problem, but I can't walk around all day with no clothes!"

"Oops, sorry Princess," Ernie mumbled as he lightly tapped me on my head.

CHAPTER 3

A warmth and golden glow suddenly washed over me, bathing me from head to toe and then disappeared as abruptly as it started. In its wake, I was wearing a pair of brown shorts with a brown midriff top. My feet and legs were encased in soft, supple boots that ran to just above my knees. Around my waist was a slim black belt with a small, elegant sword of blue on one side and its accompanying knife of red on the other side. The most amazing thing though, as I looked over my shoulder, I could see that I now had wings just like Ernie. As I shrugged my shoulders, I could feel the wings flex open and closed. I walked over to Ernie's water bowl to admire my new wings, when I found that there had been a few other changes. My blonde hair was now fire red as were my formerly blue eyes. Definitely made for one weird reflection, I thought.

A low rumble of contentment came from across the small pool where I had dropped Mr. Blue. He had changed back into his huge, fuzzy, goblin-eating self. As he rolled and stretched on the ground like a bear just emerging from a long winter's sleep, the thought ran across my mind that maybe this wasn't a dream after all. I began to consider that I might be in real trouble after all.

"There now, you look like the Princess I used to know," laughed Ernie. "Now you should have all your powers back."

With a flick of my hand toward some nearby rocks, a large ball of flame engulfed and melted them to ash. Well, that was a lot better than the little balls of flame I had been shooting before. Then I realized what the big lizard had said, "What do you mean I look the same now as before."

"You really don't know who you are, do you Princess?" Ernie grumbled with a puzzled look on his face. "This isn't how it was supposed to be when you came back. This is most puzzling, Princess!"

"Okay, how about you pretend I don't know anything about myself and give me the skinny on who or what I am, you overgrown iguana. Cause it's starting to peeve me off that everyone but me is in on who I am."

"But Princess, I told you I'm not an iguana, whatever that is, but a royal dragon!" whined Ernie.

"ERNIE!" I yelled while I stomped my foot into the hard ground and gave the look of scorn that usually had people running for cover. (My temper is well known back home, wherever that was).

"All right Princess, as you wish," grumbled Ernie. "But I'm not a lizard or this iguana thing," he mumbled under his breath just loud enough for me to hear. "Princess a long time ago . . ."

"Yeah, yeah I know in a galaxy far, far away," I sniped.

"No Princess, right here in this world," Ernie said with a puzzled look on his face.

Giving a small chuckle, I told the confused dragon, "Don't worry about it, Ernie, I guess Stars Wars hasn't made it here."

"Anyways as I was saying, this world was ruled by Queen Ellie. She had four daughters, each of whom was to rule one fourth of the kingdom after her death. Each of these daughters had a different father, who each had the power of one of the four elements in our world. As Ernie started this story, he settled himself down in the sun, curling his tail around his body and folding his wings onto himself. "The first daughter had power over the wind, the second the power over earth, the third over water, with the fourth, and the youngest, the power over fire."

"Hmmmm sort of like me, you mean?"

"No Princess, exactly like you," Ernie scowled. "The queen, not only being a not-so-great ruler, was an even worse mother. Each daughter was placed in a castle in the four different parts of the kingdom they were to rule at a year old. There they were raised and taught how to use their powers by tutors who knew something of the subject."

"And who was my tutor?"

With a proud shake of his large head and small smile, Ernie answered, "Me, your Princess, I was your tutor, of course." As Ernie settled back down, he continued with his tale. "Now where, were we? Oh yes, well about fifteen years ago the youngest Princess, who was a very curious little girl wanted to learn not only her own power, but that of all her sisters for she loved to learn, just for the joy of learning."

With a shake of his head, Ernie dipped his head into his water bowl for a quick drink. "Sorry Princess, I am so used to being on my own and not talking this much."

"That's all right, back home I'm usually the one that's doing all the talking."

"Yes, I remember that about you, but getting back to the story. The other sisters learned what the youngest wanted to do, and because each was jealous of their own powers and guarded these powers at all costs, they set out to get rid of the youngest daughter."

"Yeah, you said she wasn't that hot of a mother but didn't she try to stop them?"

Ernie looked down at the ground then back up to my face. "I am sorry to say, Princess, but the first thing the three older sisters did was to banish their mother to another world. That's when I knew that the youngest sister had to be hidden away."

"Ok let me get this straight, I'm the youngest sister, I have no mother, and three raving lunatics are after me because I like to learn stuff so someone sent me gods know where to protect me. Does that about cover it?" I asked in a sarcastic tone.

With a big, proud smile Ernie shook his head and beamed "Why yes, Princess, you got it right."

Man, this big lizard didn't know sarcasm when it hit him head on. Squatting down on some rocks by Ernie, it was starting to really, really sink in that I might be in a whole lot more trouble than I had thought before. I was hoping maybe that this had all been a bad dream after all and I'd wake up from it sooner rather than later. "Ok Ernie, so tell me who my father was."

"Well, Princess, I don't know exactly who your father was. But I do know that he was a demon."

"Well that's just peachy, there's some more great news!" I huffed. "So if I was hidden away somewhere, then how did I get back here?"

"All I can think is that one of your sisters found you and somehow bought you back to our world. That shift you were wearing with the mark was to keep you from doing magic until you fell into their hands, I would guess, Princess."

"And what about Mr. Blue turning from a teddy bear into a monster, Ernie?" as my big, furry buddy ambled over to me with that lost puppy dog look on his face. Reaching up, I absently gave the big fur ball a quick pat on his belly, getting a giant purr out of my new, old friend.

"Oh, that's simple, Princess, he is a lesser demon, your protector. When someone goes through from our world to yours, they take on a different form. In fact, when you go through to another world, you never know what form you're going to take.

"He swallowed a receptacle that held your power to keep it safe from harm, as well, Princess." "Yeah, Ernie, I found that, it was totally gross by the way. On the bright side, I guess it could have been worse, it could have come out the south end of him."

Sitting quietly, all three of us lost in our own thoughts, I was trying to take in all the new information on my life in this world and reconciling that with the one that I had back home. Now I seemed to better understand why I had always felt alone and like I never fit in with anyone. The strange dreams I had as a kid about dragons, and castles, and the feeling of freedom while flying through the air. Guess those weren't so much dreams as repressed memories. What bothered me the most was who was I really? Was I the person in this world or the person in the other world? Learning that my father was a demon and my mother was a wicked queen, was not good. Not good at all.

"Princess, you look like something is bothering you?"

"Yeah, Ernie, not too sure who I'm supposed to be right now; just the average geeky girl who went to bed last night or the half wicked demon who woke up in a different world today. Plus having a wicked mother and a demon father doesn't say much for my personality, does it?"

"Princess, I have lived a thousand years and one thing I know above all else in this world is that it is not the heritage that makes the person, but what that person does with what is inside them. Each person has it in them to be bad or good in their life, and in turn treat others with hatred or kindness." Cocking his head to the side and giving me a stern look, Ernie chuckled. "Besides, Princess, anyone I taught would never dare turn out bad."

Rising up and sniffing the air, Ernie looked around then looked back at me with concern. "My Princess, I suggest that we leave this area before we are found by your sister's goblin soldiers."

CHAPTER 4

Urg was big for a goblin. He stood at least six feet tall and had arms that looked like they were wrapped in steel, and stood on two legs the size of tree trunks. His mighty tusks were embedded with the many jewels of the vanquished foes he had fought over the years in his rise to lead Princess Rli's goblin army. Rli, the princess who controlled the element of earth reigned over all that lived in these mountains, and all those whom she controlled lived in fear of Rli, even Urg. Right now, especially Urg!

As she watched through slitted eyes, the commanders of her army marched into her dark throne room. She could see and smell the fear of failure drifting off their bodies in the flickering torch light. As they halted before her throne, the goblins fell to their knees trembling, not so much out of respect as in fear for their meager lives.

"WELL?!" Rli yelled in a booming voice that surprisingly issued from the slight figure that sat high on an earthen throne. Her voice infuriated her two pets. Both were giant cousins of the lizards used by the goblins to track down slaves or others that displeased Rli and they shared the sour temperament of their princess.

"M-m-my Princess," Urg started in a quaking voice, giving each of the princess' pets a quick glance. "We have searched for your sister all the way to the dark woods, and have found no trace of her. In fact, I have lost several of my men and . . ."

With a flick of her hand, suddenly Urg stopped talking and, with a look of complete surprise frozen on his face, he turned into what looked like solid rock before the other goblins.

"I am not interested in who or how many men you lose," Rli now stood and glared down on the rest of the quivering group gathered below the throne the Princess stood before. "You!" she pointed at the next biggest goblin in the group. "You are the new commander of my army and you will find my sister, no matter the cost."
"Yes, my Princess," mumbled the new (very reluctant) goblin leader. "We think that she is traveling with Ernie, the dragon, back home to her castle."

"Then send out all the troops, for I want my little sis brought back to me in one piece and that cursed interfering dragon's head for mounting on my wall."

"As you wish, my Princess," and the goblins all bowed to their princess and, with furtive glances at their former leader, backed to the exit.

"See that you don't fail me or you will be my pets' next chew toy." As the group quickly filed out of the throne room, they could hear the maniacal laughter of their princess, and the slithering bodies of her pets as they approached their new chew toy, and the goblins' former commander.

Soon runners were seen rushing from the castle in all directions, like an anthill disturbed by a naughty child. They were looking for any trace of the two fugitives from Princess Rli. For each goblin knew failure was not an option in this land ruled by their mad princess.

———————

Hanging on tightly, with my eyes closed, to two protruding scales on Ernie's back, feeling the rush of wind flow through my hair and down my back, one had to reflect on how far I'd come in the last few days and surprised that I would be riding on the back of a talking dragon. Only two days ago, I would have been petrified to think of flying on an airplane, you know a nice, safe enclosed metal tube flying thousands of feet in the air. Yet here I am, flying barely above the ground, dipping into valleys, and across lakes like some errant heat seeking missile.

Of course, reflecting back on the two little green goblins that found us in Ernie's home, they didn't leave me much choice in escape routes. Along with the surprise of seeing Ernie gulp both little guys down like a mid morning snack, I guess I wasn't fully thinking at the time. "Uhm, Ernie I thought you don't eat people," I stammered.

"I don't eat people." Ernie gave me a wide grin, "those were goblins."

"Yeah, well, half demons are people too, right?"

"Well, of course, Princess." Ernie let out a small belch. "Oh, excuse me Princess, goblins sit heavy on the stomach, don't you agree?"

"Uhm yeah, Ernie, sure, I'll have to take your word for that." Looking around for more goblins or their little lizard pets, I wondered what would happen next in this crazy place. I didn't have to wait for long before Ernie suggested that I hop on his back for a ride back to my old home. "Well how about Mr. Blue, can you carry both of us?"

"Mr. Blue can come with us, no problem," Ernie said, lightly thumping his upset stomach. "Just snap your fingers and he will revert back to your teddy bear, snap them again, and he will be back as a demon."

"Oh, well big guy back to small fuzz ball size." Snapping my fingers, sure enough Mr. Blue was back to being my old raggedy blue buddy. Tucking Mr. Blue into my shorts, and crawling up on Ernie's back, I held tight onto two protruding scales not expecting the rush of a ride I would soon have.

"Ready, Princess? Here we go, hang on tight." With a quick leap and a snap of his mighty wings, we were swiftly gliding through the mountains on our way to my old castle. Just thinking about everything that had happened to me so far was so weird for a girl that led a dull life back home. The one little thing that still bothered me was the greedy look Ernie gave me after eating those two little goblins. Sort of like he wasn't quite being fully truthful about eating demons or others for that matter, and did he seem a little nervous when I grabbed the hilt of the small sword at my side? A girl could really think she had fallen down a rabbit hole, the way things were going around here.

Ernie turned his head slightly to the right, jarring me out of my reflective mood and yelled back at me, "Princess, I am going to land by the shore of this lake for the night."

"All right, Ernie," I yelled while giving him a good couple of whacks on his back so he knew that I had heard him.

As we hit the shoreline, Ernie circled the beach then landed as gracefully as he had taken off. With him bending close to the ground, I slid off his back and peered around at our new rest stop. We were in a small green valley with a lake in the middle, surrounded by a grove of those great fruit trees that I have seen all over this strange place. It was peaceful and serene, but I was beginning to distrust first impressions in this new home of mine.

"Ernie, I am going to gather something to eat," I said, heading off to the woods to be by myself for a couple of minutes. I wanted to get a better look at that little pig sticker I wore around my waist and see why it made Ernie nervous when he thought I was going to pull it out when those goblins showed up.

"Well Princess, I don't think . . .," Ernie stammered.

"Yeah, well Ernie, I am the princess around here, so you say. So don't sweat the small stuff, just rest, I won't go far." By then I was slipping into the woods, peering around for any danger. After a couple of minutes, when I was satisfied I was far enough away from Ernie, I pulled my sword from its scabbard to check out what I had. It was a thin bladed little sticker with a gold handle. The blade itself seemed to have a light blue shine, almost the color of ice; in fact, touching the blade lightly I could feel a wintry shiver run up my arm as though putting my fingers in a tub of freezing water.

Looking at my new toy, I was bought back to my surroundings by a small snap of twigs in the woods in front of me. "Who's there?" I called, lighting a small ball of flame in my hand. I noticed that it was starting to get dark and was thinking maybe I should head back to the lake. Another snap in front of me caught my attention again. "Who's there? If you don't come out, I'll fry your butt!"

"Please don't hurt me," squeaked a voice that issued out of the skinny little body that stepped out of the woods in front of me. Before me stood a little guy about three and a half feet tall with a scraggly beard and a big head of fluffy hair. He was wearing what looked like a pair of raggedy pants and his shirt didn't look to be in much better condition. As I stepped closer to get a better look at him, I could tell that the little guy was a bit ripe, well, maybe a lot ripe. My nose wrinkled from the odor rising in the air from his unwashed body.

"It's ok, I won't hurt you," I said, while taking a few short steps upwind from my new visitor. "Just who and what are you?"

"Well, I am a troll, and my name is Scom. What are you?"

"Nice to meet you, Scom. Everyone tells me that I am the fire princess. I guess I'm a demon from what my companion tells me, I can't remember my old name, and I'm having a really bad couple of days here. In fact, I keep thinking I am going to see a white rabbit hop by any second now."

"Well, is he good to eat, Princess?"

"Is who good to eat?"

"Why, this white rabbit thing, Princess."

"Never mind about the rabbit, Scom, I should be getting back to the lake."

"Well, I didn't bring up the rabbit, and I am hungry, but of course trolls are always hungry, are fire princesses always hungry? 'Cause I know I'm always hungry, Princess. You understand though, right Princess?"

"Yes, I understand Scom," I was now slightly regretting the urge I had had to find out who was lurking in the woods. Putting my sword back in her home, I turned and headed back toward the lake, slowly picking some fruit off the trees I passed. As I walked back, my newfound friend tagged along and was chattering away about what he had been doing when I found him in the trees. Suddenly something Scom had been chattering about finally registered. "What did you just say, Scom, about a dragon flying toward the water princess' castle?"

"Well, just, Princess, it seems funny that a dragon should be flying away from their home, and flying toward Princess Chell's castle on the shore. I mean dragons don't like water, and Princess Chell doesn't like fire so, you know it just seems strange is all. You understand, right Princess?" Getting an inquisitive look on his face, Scom whispered, "Say you didn't fly in with that dragon, did you Princess?"

"Hush, Scom, I need to think for a second!"

"Well, I was just wondering, because you're carrying a dragon slayer sword on you and everyone knows that a dragon slayer sword is the only thing that will kill the flame or heart of the dragon. So are you a dragon slayer, Princess, just asking, because you understand, right Princess, because I just saw a dragon and . . ."

"Ok, enough Scom. Just be quiet for a second, please."

"Oh yes, Princess, when someone tells me quiet, I can be quiet, I was just . . ."

Maybe it was the look I threw at Scom, or just common sense finally breaking through the little troll's head, but he stopped in mid-sentence and soon found a tree to sit under. While he wasn't totally quiet, I could hear him mumbling under his breath, it was quiet enough for me to think about what I had just learned from the little guy. Thinking that Ernie, my former tutor may have reasons for doing what he was doing, I figured that sitting here worrying wasn't going to get me anywhere and the best thing to do was to go right to the source and find out what was going on.

"Come on, Scom, we are going to go find a dragon and get some answers to some questions."

CHAPTER 5

As we came back to the beach, I noticed that a still mumbling Scom had fallen behind me, as if shielding himself from what was lurking ahead. "Ernie," I called out, noticing that the dragon was lying down with his eyes closed. "Ernie, are you up?"

"Oh it's you, Princess," Ernie rumbled as he raised his nose and took a sniff of the air. "Princess, why do you smell like troll, especially like a really stinky, little troll?"

"Well, Ernie, I don't smell like a troll, this troll smells like a troll," I laughed as I pulled a reluctant Scom in front of me, which also happened to coincide with the watering of my eyes from the smell of the little guy. Yeah, this little dude was definitely ripe, and ready for a wash and rinse.

Scom gave a little indignant cry, "HEY, I will have you know that I just fell in the lake two months ago, and it wasn't even time for my bath! I'm a troll, we don't do baths or at least not much!"

"Yeah, we can tell, troll. Princess, we need to get rid of this troll. Not only do they smell, but they are trouble wherever they go." Ernie huffed, with a superior look on his face.

"Well, at least we aren't like dragons, going around eating and burning, or is it burning and then eating, well

26

you understand, Princess, right? Say dragon, you didn't happen to eat my relatives over in the dark forest two years ago, did you dragon?" Scom asked as he gave Ernie a searching look. "I mean, all you dragons look alike when one is running from your fire breath; talk about stink, I . . ."

"Ok, enough you two. Let's settle down for the night and get some sleep. We will talk about this in the morning." Finding a small pile of leaves under a tree, I threw myself down to get some shut eye, my hunger gone, and my mind in turmoil with all the stuff flowing through it. Soon though, with the quiet breathing of my two companions, I was almost asleep when it hit me. I still wanted to know my true name. "Ernie, ERNIE, wake up!"

"What is it, Princess?" Ernie asked groggily.

"My true name, what is it? I don't even know it."

"I am sorry, Princess, your mother never named any of her daughters until their fifteenth birthdays. What was your name in your other life, Princess, your other world?"

"I just remembered, it was Ceri," I told Ernie.

"Then that is your name here Princess. Princess Ceri. Now we need a good night's sleep, for it will be a long day tomorrow," Ernie said as he lay his head back down. He was soon snoring.

"Yeah, good night, Ernie," I sighed trying to find a comfortable place on the bed of leaves I was lying on. Closing my eyes, I promised myself that tomorrow I would get answers from my stubborn dragon companion.

Sig knew they were close now. His group had been running down the dragon and Princess like only goblins could. Some of his men, the weak ones, had fallen out on the trail and disappeared. No matter how many goblins he had, when they caught up with the two ahead, he would have enough to finish the job. The dragon thought he could lose them by flying away. He had forgotten that the goblins had other trackers, trackers that flew the night sky. Yes, Sig thought, we will have them tomorrow, the next day for sure. As he spurred his men on, Sig thought of the nice tasty dragon steaks his men would soon enjoy, and who knew, maybe after Rli was done with her sister, some good demon meat too.

Stretching on my make-shift bed, I wondered what had woken me from my short sleep. It could have been the breeze blowing through the leaves of the tree I was lying under, or the birds chirping in the brush at my feet. Or the splashing and yelling that was coming from the lake. "Oh, crap." With the sound finally registering, definitely a creature in distress, I hopped up and ran to the edge of the lake. The sight that greeted my eyes was both comical and pathetic at the same time.

Ernie was at the edge of the lake, dunking what looked like a load of dirty laundry. Except this pile of dirt and mud was fighting and yelling in a small squeaky voice. "ERNIE! STOP IT, LET SCOM UP!" I yelled, flicking a small ball of flame at the dragon to get his attention.

"Oh Princess, I was just giving our little friend a bath here," as he let the small, thoroughly soaked bundle of troll come up for air. "I just thought it would make it better for you, if you didn't have troll stink hanging in the air for breakfast."

"You mean you didn't want your breakfast to stink, dragon," squeaked the sopping wet little troll.

"Ernie, you just leave him alone, and go get us some breakfast, please," I demanded as I helped the little guy out of the water.

"Oh yes, as you say, Princess." As he walked away from the lake, his tail flicked around and accidentally knocked the little guy back into the lake. At least, I took it as an accident, because right now I wasn't too sure where Ernie's friendship lay. The one thing I did need now was friends I could be sure of.

"Come on Scom. Let's get you out of this lake and on dry land." Well one thing I was sure of about the little guy was that the soaking that Ernie had given him had definitely helped improve the smell around here, no matter the dragon's motives.

As the two of us walked back to the trees, Scom was very quiet, which in our short time together seemed out of character for the little guy. "What's on your mind, Scom, why so quiet?"

"I don't think that dragon is looking out for you, Princess, please be careful. I think I was supposed to be breakfast before you woke. You understand, right Princess?"

"Yeah, Scom, I'm beginning to think that too."

He gave me a small grin as we entered the tree line, but it quickly disappeared as soon as we came upon Ernie setting out our breakfast in the small clearing we had spent the night in. "Aah here you are, my friends. Your breakfast is ready, my Princess," Ernie said, while giving a sly look at Scom.

"Fine, thanks Ernie, it looks good." While sitting down and munching our way through breakfast, I figured it was the best time to bring up some questions I had. "Hey Ernie, since I have wings does that mean I can fly?"

"Yes Princess, you can fly, it's like anything else you do; just like throwing a spear. Your mind thinks what you're going to do and your arm muscles just do what needs to be done. You just think of flying and then your wings will make you fly."

"So I just step up and want to fly and, WHOA!" As my wings popped out, I was suddenly flapping a few feet off the ground, just as natural as could be. Even a girl afraid of heights could get used to this! As I lifted higher in the air and swooped down on the two below me, I figured this could become a fun habit to get into and it sure as heck beat walking everywhere all the time.

Landing again with Scom clapping, jumping around, and Ernie scowling at us, I figured it was time to regain a little of my princess airs back again and finish up breakfast so we could get on the move again. "So Ernie, just where was it you said we were headed?"

"Why to your old home," Ernie purred with a quick glance at me. "It's just over these hills a day or two more of flying."

Over to the side, where Ernie couldn't see him, I could see Scom slowly shaking his head with a worried look on his face and then nodding in the opposite direction. "But you know, I was just thinking that maybe I'm not ready to go home yet, Ernie," I said, as I gave him a piercing glance.

"Princess, you should think of all the people who would be glad to see you again." As he was speaking, I noticed that he was slinking closer to me with each word he uttered. "I must insist that you go home now, Princess."

"No Ernie, I think Scom is right. I don't think it would be a great idea to go with you right now."

"THAT LITTLE TROLL, I'LL TEACH HIM TO INTERFERE!" Ernie yelled and reared up looking for the cause of his troubles. "I should've eaten that little snack last night!"

As he cast side to side looking for the cause of his sudden rage, I could see Scom inching closer to me through the weeds. I pulled my sword, thinking that I needed to keep Ernie's attention on something other than the frightened little troll he was looking for.

"Ernie," I whispered. I don't know if it was my quiet voice or the blue blade in my hand, but I had Ernie's full attention for the moment.

"Princess, what's with the sword, we are friends, aren't we?" he whispered slyly.

"I'm beginning to wonder about that, Ernie. Right now I would like to know why you want to take me somewhere besides my castle?"

"It's that little troll, Princess; I know he's been filling your head with . . ."

"Cut it, Ernie. I know bullpoop when I hear it, and right now you're spilling a ton of it each time you open your mouth."

"All right Princess, you win. I was paid to tutor a little demon brat, but your sister Erie paid better. I was to get rid of you and if you ever came back, I was to deliver you to her."

"So you weren't really my friend? Was all that a fake?"

"Me? A friend with a little demon half breed? PLEASEEEE! I am a royal dragon, not a nursemaid," so saying Ernie rose to his full height then dived down to catch Scom who had, by this time, moved to my side. "You little trouble maker, I'll teach you to interfere with your betters . . ."

As Ernie reached out for my little informer, I slashed under his chin, catching him along the neck and slicing down his chest. The effect of the dragon sword cut Ernie's words off in mid sentence. As I watched the dragon, he turned into an instant dragon popsicle. The morning sun glittered off the ice sculpture of the dragon, like a mountain of diamonds.

Walking up and leaning on the icy cold leg of my former

tutor, Scom gave a little shake of his head. "Well, I guess that takes care of him. You understand, right Princess?" Just then there was a creak and I watched as tons of ice slowly fell to shatter in a million tiny bits. "Oops, sorry Princess," Scom said while looking over the mess he had just created in our little clearing, with a look of contrition his face.

"That's all right, Scom. Now I just have to figure where I can go from here."

"Uh Princess . . ."

"Hush Scom, I really need to think," I said, sitting down on a small stump in the middle of the clearing.

"But Princess, I think . . ."

"Scom, I know you want to help, but we need to, oh darn!" As I looked up to scold Scom, I noticed that we weren't alone in the clearing anymore. The whole edge of the woods was full of goblins, some with wicked looking swords and spears. Others with what looked like cross bows – all aimed at Scom and me.

One big mean-looking fellow, with a broken tusk on one side of his smile, stepped forward and pointed at Scom. "Move an inch, Princess, and we will make your friend into a pin cushion with our bolts."

If I had been by myself, I would have thrown Mr. Blue out into the middle of the clearing and snapped my fingers. Between my sword and my big fuzzy protector, I would have taken my chances. But with the little troll just standing there, I couldn't risk getting my new friend hurt.

"Very nice, Princess. Now put away your sword and slowly unbuckle the belt, and throw it over to me," said the big, green ugly.

Not much choice, I guess. "All right, just chill out and

don't hurt my friend." So I reluctantly did what I was told, while all the time trying to figure a way out of this latest mess. This really was not turning out to be my week in this new place, and I was really beginning to miss my old, boring home, wherever that was from here. "Now, let my friend go, I did what you wanted."

"No Princess, I think we will keep him around for insurance." As the big bully stepped forward, I just caught the glimpse of a fist aimed at my face. Before everything went dark, I could hear Scom cry out and the goblin's nasty laugh about the rich rewards they were going to get when they got home.

CHAPTER 6

Sig was in a good mood for a goblin. He had seen the dragon destroyed; the Princess was captured (along with a nice little troll morsel). He was almost home with no trouble so far. All his group had to do was get across this lowland area, this cursed little green valley, and then they were home free. This was the place that he had lost most of his men while chasing the Princess and her group, but he would just have to keep a better eye on his soldiers going back. Of course to Princess Rli, it didn't matter how many men he lost as long as she got hold of her sister, that's why Sig knew it was important not to come back home empty-handed.

It was the bumping that woke me up. Hanging over the shoulder of a goblin, while he was running cross country isn't the most comfortable ride a girl could have. Of course, it didn't help that I was traveling like a trussed up game trophy. After what seemed like a lifetime of being bumped around, my large, ugly, green transportation gave a great grunt and heaved me to the hard ground. As my butt slammed down on the rocks, my first thought was that that was no way to treat a princess. The second thought was to find Scom and make sure that he was all right and hadn't become a goblin snack.

"Psssst, Princess over here," came a slight little whisper behind me. I rolled over and was greeted by the sight of the little troll, still alive, and none the worse for the wear except for being in the same state of restraint as me. The one silver lining in this situation was that as I rolled over I could still feel Mr. Blue stuffed in my shorts where I had last left him. I figured these goblins must not know about my fuzzy friend so he could be the ace in the hole for getting us out of here, when and if the situation presented itself.

The biggest of the goblins, who I took as the leader of this little expedition came over to where we were lying and gave us cold stare. "All right Princess, from here on out you and your little partner will walk. I need my men as guards, not as porters of princesses and trolls."

As he reached down to cut the ties with a wicked looking knife, he gave me a lopsided one- tusked grin, "Just remember, Princess, any wrong move on your part, the troll will pay the price." Reaching over and then cutting the ropes on Scom's legs, the bully patted him on the head, "and it's been so long since I've had troll stew." Laughing, he walked away from us, back to the merry little band of goblins he was in charge of.

Soon one of the other goblins walked over and threw some kind of black bread, fruit, and a drink bottle down at our feet. Well, I guess this wasn't going to be a formal sit down dinner. I helped Scom sit up and divided up the food while our new guard gave a small belch, snickered and then settled down on a rock to keep an eye on us. Guess manners aren't high on a goblin's list of things to learn as they grow up.

I noticed that Scom had a worried look on his face, at

least more worried than usual so I tried to cheer the little guy up some. "Look Scom, it's not as bad as it seems, and I won't let them eat you, no matter what they keep saying, okay?"

"I'm not worried about the goblins, Princess. I think they will be dead tomorrow," he whispered as he chowed down on his portion of our supper.

"Oh, well okay then, then what are you worried about, and why do you think they will be dead tomorrow?" I asked as I nibbled on my bread and fruit. I had taken a quick drink from the water bottle and found that it was some sour tasting beer concoction. If this was what goblins drank all the time, I could not only see why they were so ugly but always in such a sour mood too.

"This valley, Princess, we will travel through tomorrow; I don't think that the goblins will make it to the other side. I worry because we may not make it there either."

"What is there? Some big bad magic down there or something?" I gave a small laugh, trying to lighten up the little troll's mood.

"Yeah magic, Princess, bad magic for goblins and uninvited guests to this valley."

Scom wouldn't look me in the eye as he said this and after he finished eating, he rolled over and went quietly to sleep which seemed a little odd for the little guy. Well whatever it was down there, it apparently was an enemy to the goblins, so maybe it could be a new friend to us. As I sat watching the night sky and the stars that had come out, I noticed that not all the goblins were too happy to be crossing this valley either. Paying closer attention, I learned that half of this band had been lost while crossing the other way through this valley, and most were apprehensive about making the return trip.

The leader, who I learned was called Sig, finally had

enough belly-aching from his men and lopped the head off the loudest protester. Talk about overreacting! After some more yelling and gesturing, the group seemed to be settling down for the night. Sig posted some guards and the camp quieted down in a tense silence. I rolled around on the rough ground 'til I found a comfortable depression that fit my body. My last thought as I drifted off to an uncomfortable sleep was that, hopefully, tomorrow would give us a chance to escape from our captors.

Silently he glides though the long grass, looking at the camp that lies before the entrance to his home. He sniffs the air, smelling the stink of the goblins, those spoilers and destroyers of all things good. He stops and concentrates on a sweeter smell in the air, something different mixed in with . . . troll. But this new smell is something else, it's like the warmth of a fire on a cold winter's night. He shakes his head and moves silently toward his prey, stalking one of the outer guards in this invasion of his lands. He crouches and waits 'til the guard turns his back. With a silent leap and a quick shake of his huge head, he easily snaps the goblin's neck like a dry twig. As he pulls the lifeless body into the bush, now we will see if my little surprise keeps them out of my valley, he thinks. If not, this is one band of travelers that will not make it out of my home in one piece, he vows.

CHAPTER 7

Opening my eyes, I can see that the goblins are starting to wake up. The kick in the side from one of my captors rouses me from my thoughts. I wake Scom up, hoping to get this day started. I wonder if I will be around when someone teaches these guys some manners. Don't they know it's not nice to kick a girl out of bed first thing in the morning, especially a princess? "HEY, big ugly, how about letting me get a drink of water and letting a girl have a little privacy for a squat before we head out to wherever we're headed to."

Sig gives me a nasty look, "Just remember, Princess, what will happen to your friend if you try to escape."

"Yeah, yeah, I get it already blah, blah, blah. You know you sound like some of my old school teachers, they didn't trust me much either."

Sig pointed at two of the bigger goblins in the group and we headed down the trail which led to the opening of the big, bad valley we were to cross today. I stopped at a small stream that crossed the path. Thinking to get rid of that awful taste in my mouth from that beer we had last night, I cupped some water in my hands to drink. Looking up, I first noticed what looked like a goblin looking at me over the tall grass on the other side of the little stream. The second thing I noticed was that the goblin in question seemed to be missing the rest of his body, and that his head seemed to be stuck on a pole on the side of the path we were to traverse today, this was definitely not a good way to start the day – especially for the goblin staring back at me.

Taking a step back and to the side of the path, I could see that I hadn't noticed that the whole path seemed to be lined with goblin heads all stuck on poles. Guess someone was trying to send a message to Sig about taking another way home. If he was smart, I hoped he might take the hint given. Unfortunately, I didn't give Sig much credit for brains, even though as I thought about it, he was smart enough to capture me.

With much shouting from my guards, the rest of the goblins gathered together and more grumbling soon ensued between them. From what I gathered, they had found their missing friends and they weren't too happy with their state of being. Of course, can't say I was too thrilled about the little display either. I felt a little tug at my side. Looking down, I saw Scom had a grim look in his eyes. "See Princess, bad place. You understand now, right Princess?"

"Yeah I understand, Scom, but I don't think Sig is going to give us much choice in the matter. We go where he tells us 'til we can escape from the big, green ugly."

I finished up my little squat duties without much privacy since Sig didn't want anyone going out on their own again.

After a quick head count, we found that only one of the guards was missing, it being the head that I had first spotted across the stream. This left twenty of the goblins to take me back to my sister. Sig soon had us moving on the trail, following the gruesome spectacle of his former men. The sight seemed to anger the goblins, not so much because of loyalty to the deceased goblins as that they like to think of themselves as masters of all that surrounds them, and they couldn't fathom something doing this to them.

As we descended into the beautiful valley, Sig had his men split up into two groups of eight with Scom and I walking in the middle of them. The other four goblins were split out to the right and left of the main groups, just off the path in outrider fashion. We moved through most of the morning in this fashion, and soon the tension of the goblins for action seemed to wane some as the day wore on.

The valley we were walking in was wider than it looked and I could see that it would take more than a day or two to cross it. I guess it is surprising how far you can get when you fly dragon express. The grasslands we were moving through were about chest high, and surrounded by small woods, with little streams and lakes. The day was very nice with the sun shining, but cooled with a slight breeze flowing down the valley floor, making the grass wave like we were skimming through the ocean. What was surprising was that there was no noise from animals or birds, almost as if they were holding their breath to see what the next act in this play was going to be.

About noon Sig called a halt for a rest and the two goblins on our left flank came in to where we had stopped. After yelling and getting no response from the other two goblins, Sig had two of his nastier looking guys keep an eye on Scom and I while the rest of them moved off to the right to check for the two missing soldiers. As I heard Sig and his group stomp around in the grass, I noticed what looked like two golden eyes peering from the grass in the other direction. With a roar, a dark brown striped blur flashed onto the path and with swipes of paws the size of dinner plates, both goblin soldiers were laying on the ground. Unfortunately for them, each was lying in about four different pieces.

Before Scom and I could move, we were once more surrounded by Sig and his goblins and the dark blur had disappeared as fast as it had arrived. Sig was not a very happy camper, and neither were any of his men. Seemed that not only had they lost two of their own just now, but they couldn't find any trace of the two that had been out on the right flank. Guess we were down now to seventeen goblins plus Scom and I. The way it was going, it didn't look like there would be enough of us left to walk out of this little valley.

—————————————

Sig soon got us started going again, except this time he had all his men grouped around the two of us. I guess he figured that there was safety in numbers, yeah right. About an hour later, we were walking when the front of the group came to an abrupt halt. Standing in the middle of the path was a huge bear. The color of its fur changed from black to brown depending on how the sun filtered through the leaves onto its body. It was massive, at least eight feet tall with paws the size of sewer covers. It just stood there in the middle of the path, on two legs that were as large as barrels, watching the goblins trying to decide how they were going to get around this huge road block.

Looking at the magnificent creature that was the cause of our unscheduled rest stop, I had this feeling that I was being watched from the side. Slowly looking over, I could see two golden eyes staring out from the grass at me again. These eyes were golden brown, with a cat-like appearance, but with something like human intelligence behind them also. As I lost myself in the hypnotic stare of those magnificent eyes, one of the goblins noticed the object of my attention. He started and gave a loud shout.

With his shout, pandemonium broke out. The huge golden streak hiding in the bushes leaped into the middle of the back group of the goblins. There were snarls of fury, yells of pain, and yuck!! Can you say goblin guts splattering about the clearing? It was pretty easy telling who was getting the better of whom, with all the goblin body parts lying about.

Sig and his men in the front group forgot about the bear in the path and turned to fight the blur of fury that was destroying the others. Big mistake, for no sooner had they turned their backs than the bear moved in with a swiftness that belied his size. Soon all there was standing was Sig, Scom, and I with our two rescuers?

I finally got a good look at the streak of destruction that had so decimated the goblins. It was a tiger, but not like a tiger that I had ever seen before. Where a tiger would be orange and black, it was a shade of golden brown with darker brown stripes on its body. Of course, that is where it wasn't covered in goblin blood. Where the white is on a tiger, it was a dark charcoal grey, almost black. Its eyes, once the heat of battle calmed down, had a look that went right through you, down to your soul. It was almost like it could tell what your innermost thoughts were, and whether they were good or bad. Interesting, but creepy at the same time, I thought.

Sig slowly backed up until he was right next to Scom and I. "Whoever you creatures are, stop or I will kill the troll," Sig said pulling the troll toward him.

With what sounded like a laugh, the tiger turned his back on us. I guess Sig took this as an insult because he dropped Scom to the ground and rushed the tiger. Three things happened all at once, so quickly that it was over before it began. The huge bear gave a yell, the tiger turned in place and swiped Sig's head off his shoulders, and the fireball I had thrown at the goblin engulfed his now headless body, turning him into a charcoal briquette. With that both creatures disappeared in a flash and I was left alone in a field of goblin parts with a troll and no idea what to do next.

Finding my sword and belt in the mess our two saviors had left of the goblins, I gathered Scom up and headed down the path to find some place to wash goblin guts off of us. A little further down the path, I found a small water hole and got both of us cleaned up the best I could. Scom seemed to be in shock and wasn't much help, but then again he was quiet, so it seemed a reasonable tradeoff to me. After getting cleaned up, grabbing a drink and eating some fruit that was on the trees around us, we moved down the path 'til we found a small open area to rest in.

By this time, it had been a while since the attack and it was starting to get dark. I was beginning to get a little worried about Scom; he hadn't said a word yet about anything that had happened, and that seemed a little out of character for the little guy.

"Scom, are you all right?" Not a sound from the little guy. Yeah, this wasn't like the little chatterbox at all. "SCOM!"

"I heard you, Princess. No need to yell, just thinking is all. You understand right, Princess?"

"I can understand, Scom. What are you thinking about so hard that you've been so quiet?"

"I've just been thinking that he must have been really mad at me is all, Princess."

"Who was mad at you? Sig?"

"Why no, Princess. My master."

"Who is your master, Scom?"

"Why he is my master, Princess," Scom said as he pointed to one of the men standing under the shadows of the nearby trees.

As both men stepped from under the trees, I got a better look at each. The first man stood at least six feet tall. He wore a pair of cut off pants and no shirt. He had a shaggy beard and long hair that was just as shaggy as his beard. In fact as I looked, I could see that his whole body was covered in hair, from across his massive chest, his hanging belly, down his legs to his bare feet.

The other person is the one who caught my attention, his body was muscular, hard and the color of bronze. As the fading light hit his skin, I could see the faint lines of what looked like stripes, like tiger stripes to be exact. Looking up into his face, I saw the same haunting eyes that had stared at me from the grass before the attack on the goblins. The goblins may have been gone but I guessed we might still be in trouble after all. Seems like this day just wouldn't end.

Standing up I decided it was time to take the tiger by the tail, so to speak. "Hey thanks for saving Scom and I back there. Of course, you know we wouldn't be here if it wasn't for the goblins, right? You do know that?" After a few minutes, I thought yeah nothing but dead silence from the two, not good. Definitely the wrong thought to have right now, at least the dead part after what they did to the goblins.

The smaller of the two men looked down at Scom. "I thought I told you not to come back here for a while, troll," he said in a rough voice.

"Yes, I know, sir, but as the Princess said, we were taken by goblins. Sorry, sir."

"You know I had ought to eat you, you little trouble maker." There was a loud laugh from the bigger of the two men until the other gave him a stern look. "Don't encourage him any, Da. Remember, he took some of your stuff too."

With that the bigger man stopped laughing and shot Scom a stern look too. "Yeah I had forgotten about that, Ro."

Stepping between Scom and the two men, I tried to give them my fiercest look. "Now look you two, you can't just go around bullying little ones like that. He is under my protection, and as Princess what I say goes."

Both men looked at me in amusement, which needless to say, raised my ire at our two saviors. My temper continued to rise as the grins on the two faces grew. Stomping my feet, I yelled, "I DON'T SEE THAT THIS IS FUNNY AT ALL!!"

The smaller of the two men, still smiling, bowed and said, "Yes Princess, forgive our poor manners." By this time, the bigger man was laughing so loud and with such merriment that my temper and the silliness in the situation soon washed over me, and I was laughing as hard as the other two.

Soon the laughter died down and our rescuers introduced themselves. "My name is Ro," said the smaller of the two men. "This one is my brother Da," he said as he pointed to the taller of the two.

"My name is Ceri, Princess Ceri, and this is . . ."

"Yes, I know who the little troll is, Princess," Ro said while giving Scom a nasty look. "Scom used to work for my brother and I, before we banished him from our valley for being the little sneak thief he is. Didn't I, Scom?"

With the way that Scom ducked his head and looked at the ground, I could see that Ro was telling me the truth, and that my little partner and I weren't out of trouble just yet. "Yes sir, that is the truth," the little troll mumbled.

"Ro, this is not the time or place," Da said in a quiet, calming voice. "We will take them home, their enemies are ours, and the pretty little Princess needs rest."

"Fine, follow us, Princess, and see that the troll doesn't walk off with the family silver," Ro grumped.

"There was silver?" Scom suddenly perked up, his small eyes lighting up with the thought of lost loot.

"Scom!" Giving the troll a stern look, I whispered, "Now is not the time for that."

"Oh yeah, right, Princess, sorry," and with that we followed our two rescuers down a side path leading deeper into the valley that they protected.

CHAPTER 8

Once again in her dark, dank, spell room, Princess Rli was working to create evil and bend it to her will. She looks through her books, searching for a spell that will penetrate the protective magic of the valley. "Never send a goblin to do an evil princess' job, as I always say." Laughing in a nasty harsh bark, the Princess finally finds the spell she needs.

"What is it, Princess?" one of the shadows hisses as it moves into the light of the flickering torch. It is a darkness, more an absence of light than a solid form. It is a form of evil magic that has been around since the start of this world; feeding off the fears and hatred of others.

"I have found a way to get at my sister, a magic that is white and pure."

"You do realize, Princess, that if you use this you will be robbed of some of your power," the shadow whispers as she looks over the shoulder of the Princess and at the book in her hands. "I cannot guarantee what the results will be, if you use this spell."

"Well, my goblins have failed me, so let's see if all this magic you have taught me will work."

"As you wish Princess, what does the spell do?"

"It is a spell that helps rescue a family member from

grave danger."

"Your sister is not in danger, Princess, I don't understand."

"Oh, she will be in grave danger when she is attacked by one of my poison flying trackers. Then as she lay dying, I will use this spell to swoop in and rescue my poor little sister."

"Once again, Princess, I cannot . . ."

"Yes, I heard you the first time. Now back to the shadows and let me concentrate." With a flick of her wrist, the darker shadow once again faded into the night corners that inhabited the spell room. Soon a small group of flying trackers were winging from the castle toward the green valley. Each tracker carrying a dose of poison to pass onto the Princess at all cost, even to losing their lives. As with the goblins before them, each knew that failing Princess Rli meant they could never return home.

"Well here we are Princess, our home sweet home," Ro said as he gave a sweeping gesture toward a cave opening.

"It's a cave," I said, looking at the dark opening then at Ro and Da to see if they were trying to pull some joke on me. "I mean I just thought it might be something a little different is all," I stammered, trying to cover up my surprise and the awkward silence that now seemed to fill the clearing we were all standing in. "Well, I'm tired so let's all go in and get some sleep, shall we?" As I headed for the entrance to their home, the two shape shifters just quietly watched me walk by, and then followed me into their house of rock.

Once inside I forgot that we were inside a hunk of rock. The floors were smooth and in places covered with rugs and woven woods of all colors and shapes. The walls also supported woven wood hangings, along with different fabrics in bright colors. The whole place was larger and roomier on the inside than it looked at first glance from the outside. All around the room, I could see large couches with huge fluffy pillows on them, and in the middle of the room was a fire pit with a stone chimney rising to the top of the roof. All in all, it wasn't the damp hole in the ground that I thought it would be. Who knew two guys could make such a great place like this that a girl could come to like?

"Surprised Princess?" asked Ro as he moved into his home and settled on one of the big couches by the fire pit. "Bet you were thinking mud floors, garbage thrown in piles, and such."

"Yeah, well, I am a little surprised by the state of your place." Looking around, I saw Scom looking and sniffing around in the corners.

Ro noticed me and gave the little guy a nasty look. "Troll, you don't think I would be that dumb to leave anything loose where you could find it, do you?"

"Oh no, oh no, sir; just looking at the old place. You understand, right?" As he said this, I noticed that he inched closer to me as if looking for protection. I gave a sigh and patted the small troll as he wrapped himself around my leg like a lost puppy once again. Scom was so going to get us in trouble if I didn't keep an eye on the little guy.

Right about then Da threw himself on one of the other couches. "Well Princess, since you're here, grab a space and tell us your problems."

"What makes you think I have a problem?" I asked as I sank down on one of the couches and lost myself (and Scom, who was still attached to my leg), in the abundant pillows.

Da gave me a penetrating look. "Princess, if you don't have problems then you should stop hanging with goblins."

So getting comfortable, I told the two about waking up in a strange place, meeting goblins, dragons, and trolls; as well as discovering that I was someone other than who I thought I was. Oh yeah, then there was the whole half-demon magic thing to deal with. Both guys just sat and listened to my story without interruption 'til I was done spilling my guts.

Ro was the first to speak after I was done with my story. "Yeah Princess, you can't trust dragons like you used to, sort of like trolls in a way, and goblins are just pure nasty folks."

"Yeah, well thanks, but that's all you got to say about what happened to me?"

"Well, no, Princess, I guess next time be careful you don't talk to goblins, dragons or trolls." Ro said drolly. Da rolled off his couch, he was laughing so hard. I don't know if it was the incredulous look on my face or the answer that Ro gave me. I do know that he was lucky though that the look I threw him at that moment wasn't one that could kill him, as much as I wanted to shut the big lug up right then.

"Well how about shape shifters then, are they safe?" I said with as much scorn as I could put in my voice.

Ro just looked at me with a wicked grin, "Why no, princess, us shape shifters are the worst of the lot. Just ask any goblin, dragon, or troll you see." With that Da's laughter grew even louder and it became infectious enough so that soon we were all laughing or at least smiling in the case of Scom.

After the laughter died down, Da suggested that we all get some sleep, and they could figure out what they wanted to do about Scom and I in the morning. Since it had been a long day, I just decided what the heck and settled down on the big comfy couch for a night of restful sleep with the others.

Suddenly I had a bad thought, "Umm Ro, the goblins could get into your valley, well how about my sister, won't she come after me since her goblins failed?"

"Don't worry, Princess, dark magic can't be used in this valley, for some reason. That's why shifters settled here. So you should be safe from your sister, since she never leaves her castle, and sends her goblins on these little gathering missions of hers.

"Well, okay. Good night, Ro."

"Yeah, good night, Princess," Ro mumbled sleepily.

Over in the corner, buried in the pillows on the other couch, I could hear Da snoring away, with Scom shifting around and mumbling in his sleep on my couch. As the fire in the cave died down, I buried myself deeper in the couch pillows to try to find sleep tonight and let tomorrow sort out all my problems.

CHAPTER 9

Finally they had found her, tracked their prey down to
this cave. Inside, they could smell others. Two of these
others were ones that had killed their kin and goblins as
well, but tonight wasn't a night for revenge. They had their
orders, and no one disobeyed Princess Rli's orders and
lived to tell about it. As they watched the light slowly die in
the cave and the room slowly descend into darkness, they
crept through the door and up along the roof, hiding in the
shadows and biding their time. Poised to strike at their
innocent victim once all the occupants of the cave were
asleep. Each time one of the creatures on the various
couches stirred, all the trackers froze and melted into the
dark shadows until there was no more movement. They
slowly gathered over the Princess as bees to a flower,
waiting to bite and deliver their deadly gift.

They waited for the moment to strike when all was quiet
and the dark shadows covered all the corners of this cave,
and all below them were in a deep sleep. Then she woke.

It was a bad dream, one that just keeps going and you
know that you can't wake up from. A dream; no, a
nightmare, of danger and dark things in the night looking

down from above, spying on you and watching your every move, just waiting. Waiting to pounce from the dark shadows, to take you back with them to wherever such darkness or malevolence spawns.

Opening my eyes from the nightmare I was having, I sat up, looking around at the dark cave. It all seemed the same as when I fell asleep, except a little darker and chillier from having the fire die down. I still couldn't shake the feeling of doom, or creepiness that the nightmare had given me.

Hearing a slight rustling like a soft wind in some twigs, I looked around for the source of this strange sound. Finally looking up at the cave ceiling, I had the impression that the rock above me had come alive with movement. With a quick flick of my wrist, I sent a small ball of flame into the air above me to light up the shadows.

"OH CRAP!" I yelled as I rolled off the couch and out from under the mass of horror that was descending toward me from the cave roof. As I rolled away from it, I could see that both Ro and Da were up on their feet looking in all directions for the threat. Also I had the fleeting impression of Scom rolling off the couch we had so recently occupied and sliding under it for protection.

As the mass of darkness hit the couch, it separated into about a dozen individual flying, flapping nightmares on wings. Each one looked like a small winged lizard about three feet long. Besides the wicked looking claws on each foot, these little nightmares each had a set of fangs extending from their mouths that would make a cobra envious. What was really scary about these beasts was that their fangs were each dripping a black, thick liquid that I wanted nowhere near my tender anatomy.

As I came up from my roll off of the couch, I was firing off balls of flame to swat these little monsters out of the air like the pests they were. I had to be careful where I aimed as both Ro and Da had joined the fray. I could see that Ro was making great use of the spear he had, while Da had changed both his hands into bear paws and was smacking down the attackers like a fly swatter.

After a couple of frantic minutes of this, all was quiet once again in the cave. As I looked around, I could see the charred and smashed remains of our attackers littering a circle around me. Looking around, all I could think was, hmmm, I wonder who they were after. Yeah, ok, so I wasn't always at my brightest when I just wake up. I may be at my perkiest in the morning, but not always the swiftest, especially after being attacked by such gruesome beasties in the middle of the night.

I started to walk back to my couch when Scom yelled something and launched himself at me with a small knife in his hand. I was so shocked by the little troll's actions, I froze in place until I felt something hit me in the back and knock me down to the floor. I felt Scom hit me from the side and then the weight was taken off my back. Hopping up, I could see Scom lying still on the floor with his arms wrapped around one of our attackers and the knife buried in the flying lizard's motionless chest.

Rushing over, the three of us carefully checked the little troll over to see if he was hurt. Ro found where the lizard had struck Scom, and he quickly cut open the wound and begun to squeeze out the dark viscous liquid and keep it from reaching the big heart of my small savior. After a couple of seconds of this, Ro finally was getting clear blood from the wound and I was starting to get sick from the sight. Da had brought over a wrap and some leaves and applied them to the troll, who still had not moved or uttered a sound throughout their ministrations.

"Is he going to be all right?" I sighed laying Scom's head in my lap.

"I don't know, Princess; I'm not sure how much poison got into his system," said Ro looking down at the little troll with a look of admiration I hadn't seen before. "This is your sister's doing and there is no telling what kind of magic she has used."

"Let's get him up on a couch where he will be more comfortable, Princess," Da said as he slowly picked up Scom and carried him over to our former bed. He set him down tenderly and then turned to Ro. "I think maybe we aren't as safe as we think in our home and maybe I'll go keep a watch for any more surprises."

"Yeah," said Ro, "guess we don't want any more surprise visitors tonight."

A nasty cackle issued from the shadows in the corner, "Little too late for that."

Both shape shifters bravely jumped in front of me. I could hear deep growls of challenge coming from both men. "Who's there?" I whispered peeking over the wide shoulders of my two protectors.

As a darker shadow detached itself from the cave wall, it gave a nasty cackle again. "What's the matter, sister, don't you remember me?" The shadow stopped in the feeble light. "Your older sister, who has come to save my dear little sister from the poison of the night trackers, to take you home to heal you from their bite."

"She didn't get bit." Ro said.

"What do you mean she didn't get bit? Of course she did, the tracker said it bit. So, of course, she got bit." The shadow staggered a little closer to us. In the dim light I could see a slight cloaked figure, but not the face of my sister, if that was actually who this was.

"Sorry," laughed Da, "but it got the troll, not the

Princess."

"NOOOOOOOOOOO!" yelled the shadow as it was enveloped in smoke and flame and then disappeared in a flash to leave us once again alone in the shape shifter's cave. "Well that was interesting," Da quietly reflected, almost to himself.

"Umm guys, I thought she couldn't use magic in this valley?"

"No, Princess, I said she couldn't use dark magic here," answered Ro.

"There's a difference?" I asked puzzled. "I just figured magic was magic."

"Oh yeah, big difference; and if she used good magic for an evil reason in this valley she is going to pay a terrible price. You did notice her stagger there at the end before she disappeared, right? Not good, not good at all for her, Princess," said Da in a low voice.

"Well, how do we fix Scom though, guys?" I asked as we all turned to look at the quiet little troll who still had not moved a muscle or made a sound in all this time. Knowing the little troll like I do, this was starting to scare me like nothing else had since I came to this world.

"Well," said Da looking down to the ground and scuffing his feet in the rugs, "I would say we need to get rid of Princess Rli and then whatever is affecting the troll will go away, Princess."

"Okay, let's go get her, and by the way you two, the troll has a name – it's Scom," I said, looking affectionately at my little savior.

Ro gave me a searching look and said, "Da means to save the tro . . . I mean Scom, we need to get rid of your sister in a permanent way, Princess."

"Yeah, I think I got that, but I'll tell you what, she may be family, but she has done gone and peeved me off to no end. If it's a fight she wants, then it's a fight she'll get, whether you guys help me or not."

Da laughed, "Oh don't worry about us, Princess; we are always up for a good fight. We'll go with you, right brother?" Da laughed harder while thumping Ro on the back, sending him staggering across the room which was no easy feat, considering the way the younger shifter was built.

"Yeah, no problem, brother, but let's get some more sleep and figure the rest of this fight stuff out in the morning. Da and I will split the watch for the rest of the night, Princess. You get some rest and then we'll figure out what to do about your sister so we can help the tro . . . I mean Scom."

With that, Da went back out to the front of the cave and Ro started to pick up what was left of our attackers and throw them down a pit at the back of the cave that I hadn't noticed before. Moving over to our shared couch, I lay down next to Scom thinking that I was way too keyed up to fall back asleep again. I snuggled down into the couch and found Mr. Blue wrapped up in the pillows where he had fallen the last time I was asleep here. Soon, with my old friend wrapped in my arms once again, I felt myself drift off to that area of the night where you walk between being awake and asleep. Then there was just darkness without dreams.

CHAPTER 10

The smell of cooking woke me from my slumber.
Stretching out on the comfy couch, last night's activities
slowly filtered back through my mind. Giving a slight gasp,
I rolled over to check on Scom. Scom lay on the couch
where Da had put him; still as quiet as he was last night.
The guilt I felt that he had taken the bite himself to save
me washed over me like a wave hitting the rocky shore line.
As I felt remorseful tears slide down my cheeks over what
my little friend had sacrificed, I felt the big hands of Da pat
my shoulder in sympathy.

"You know Princess the tro . . ." He stopped as I gave
him a nasty look, "I mean Scom, Princess; he would not
want you sad for him," Da whispered in a contrite voice.

"Yeah, well, if it wasn't for me he wouldn't be in this
mess in the first place now would he, Da?"

"Believe me, Princess, when it comes to trolls, they
don't need a princess around to get in trouble, especially
this little one here."

"Oh?" I gave him an inquisitive look.

"Yes, Princess, trolls like Scom are thieves and gathers
of gold, silver, and jewels..."

"Yeah mostly of other people's gold, silver, and jewels,
Princess," said Ro as he walked up to the couch. "This little

one had worked for us for a year before he disappeared with some of our gold."

"Okay, but still, he did save my life last night, so he may be a thief but he is also my friend."

"Why, thank you, Princess," whispered a small voice from the middle of the couch.

"Scom!" I said as I whipped around and saw that Scom's eyes were now open; though the light in them was not as bright as before. This worried me because he had not moved from the spot he had lain in all night. I felt still more tears stain my cheeks, now though in happiness at seeing my friend awake.

"Trolls are also tough little creatures, Princess," Da said as he walked away from us, chuckling and shaking his head.

"Scom, are you okay? Can you move? Let me get you some water," I said as I scrambled around looking to do something, anything, to help my little savior.

"I'll be all right, Princess. Us trolls have thick hides and very slow blood, so it takes a lot to poison us," Scom said as he slowly sat up. "The problem is, as long as your sister is around, her magic will slowly kill me. It will take longer than for you or the shape shifters, but in the end it will affect me like everyone else."

"Well then, like I said last night, we have to get rid of her permanently. It's not like my sister's not trying to do the same to me."

"That won't be easy, Princess," whispered Scom, "but it will be necessary not only for me, but for your future safety as well."

"So the three of us must get rid of my sister then," I shrugged as I contemplated the death of a sister I never knew I had.

"No Princess, the four of us will," said Scom as he sat up straighter in the pillows with a new look of determination.

"Well actually, it will be five of us, Princess," said Ro, giving me a peculiar look. "If I remember the stories about you right, Princess, you do know you have a demon protector with you, don't you?"

"Umm yeah, what, oh you mean Mr. Blue? Oh yeah, in all the excitement I forgot. I guess I am still just so used to him being my old stuffed teddy bear. Why and how can you tell what he is?"

Da laughed. "One shape shifter can tell another no matter what form it takes; be it a tiger, wolf, bear or demon."

"Yeah," laughed Ro even harder "no matter if they're a little stuffed bear or a big stuffed bear; right, brother?"

Da stopped for a moment in thought, then laughed all the harder as he walked back over to us. "Yeah I guess you are right, brother," clapping Ro across the shoulders, with a loud slap, and sending him rolling across the cave floor.

From then on the two brothers grew serious in getting ready for the storming of my sister's castle. They packed supplies and made the plans we needed to beat my sister and rid Scom of the dark magic that was affecting him. That these plans mainly consisted of storming the castle and just kicking every butt in it didn't seem much of a plan; but heck, what did I know about this kind of stuff? I guess winging it hadn't hurt me in this world so far, so why change now?

The supplies the two made up included packs of food, clothes, rope, and other niceties we would need on the trail. Along with our packs, the two shape shifters broke out weapons so that all in the party were now fully armed. Both Ro and Da had strapped huge, long broad swords to their backs along with shields that were almost as long as they were. Each sword was double edged and took two hands for the men to use. Each shape shifter was also adorned with a helmet that was marked with their animal totem on the crest.

Seeing my puzzled look at all the armor that the two shifters had decked themselves out with, Ro said, "We use our animal totems in small fights to protect our valley, Princess, but this is war and when we go to war, we don our father's weapons. If we need them, our animals will be there for us, Princess."

Scom had picked out a double edged axe that was almost as tall as him. I was afraid that the little guy wouldn't be able to lift it, but after watching him swing the axe with no problems, I stopped worrying about him. For me, I had my sword and knife, along with my ability to barbeque any unfriendly, and my big buddy, Mr. Blue, who I had changed back into his giant sized version of a goblin eating monster, with a snap of my fingers.

"Here Princess, try these too." Da said smiling as he handed me a short, gold bow and a quiver of arrows."

"I think I have enough, don't you?"

"These arrows are from our mother and have a little magic left in them. As you pull the arrows back, just think fire and when you release them your flame magic will fly with the arrows."

"Oh cool."

"Yes, I thought you would like that," said Da with a chuckle. "It will extend the range you can reach our enemies with your flames."

"Thanks, Da."

"No problem, Princess. Always glad to help."

"Well now that we are all ready, are there any questions?" asked Ro, looking at each of us in turn. "Okay then, we should be safe until we get out of our valley, then we have a pass we need to cross and then the castle to storm. Until then, we keep together and watch each other's back. Oh and Princess, until we leave the valley stay with us on the path for your own safety, do not wander off."

"Are you expecting more goblins?"

"No Princess, but Da sent out messengers to gather other shape shifters, and they are not as civilized as us, so it would be better to stay close together. Some of the others may take you as a tasty morsel."

"Oh I see, no problem, I don't want to become someone's breakfast. Plus if nothing else, I can always fly to my sister's castle."

"Not a problem Princess, just remember we may need the help the other shape shifters can give us, and I think it would be better for all concerned if you just stick with us."

And with that we set out to storm a castle, get my little friend his health back, and kick my older sister's butt into next week for all she had done to mess with my life so far. Yeah, I could tell that this was going to be such a warm and fuzzy family reunion.

CHAPTER 11

With a puff of smoke and flame, Rli returned to her castle. As her feet hit the ground, she once again stumbled as she had in front of her sister. The dark clad shape slowly climbed the stairs to her throne, where even her pets slinked away from her dark mood; afraid of the wrath all felt steaming just below the surface of her sanity. "Dead," she croaked out in a rasp. "I want them all dead! Now! Send out everyone, all but my throne room guards. Find her and make her dead." One of her braver goblin leaders stepped forward to say something, but was struck down where he stood with a wave of her arm. "NO MORE TALK!" she screamed, and as she stood, the hood on her cloak fell back revealing her face. All of her people just sat and gasped for a second before each ran to obey her orders, more in self preservation than in obedience.

She limped over to a reflecting pool and looked down into the water to see what the magic that had gone wrong had wrought to her body. As she stared down into that pool, what little sanity she had left fled her mind. The echoes of the screams that followed spurred on any left in the castle to carry out their mistress's last orders.

The shape shifters led us back to the path we had followed earlier when we were with the goblins. Now that I didn't have to focus on escape, I could look around and see how beautiful and peaceful this little valley was. The path, at first, led through some low grass lands. For the most part the grass was about head high and hid the land about us, but soon we came to areas where the grass was shorter, and we had a spectacular view of the lands around us.

We could see small groves of trees running along the banks of quiet streams. The trees adding their shade and cool comfort to the flowing waters, along with buzz of the insects romping and flying in the grass. One could almost lose the thought that we were a group marching off to war.

Looking ahead and behind us, I could see the mountains that we had left with the goblins and the pass that our tiny group was headed for. "Not a very big valley, is it?" I observed.

"This is the short part of the valley, Princess, a crossroads of sorts. The main part extends to your left where it opens into a wider section of our valley where most everyone lives," Ro explained.

"But you and your brother have your home here, close to the path."

Da laughed, "No Princess, that little cave is only a small rest place for our kind when we need to keep an eye out on who is traveling the roads. Our real home is down in the main part of the valley. Maybe, when we are done here with this little adventure, we'll take you there to visit."

"Yeah, that would be nice. I could go for a nice, peaceful visit somewhere quiet." With a hushed sigh, I looked around. "Then what were you doing down on this end of the valley, not that I'm complaining that you were here, you understand."

Da laughed again, "We had heard that there were

dragons flying overhead and goblins with their trackers menacing our valley so we decided to come and investigate the cause of all these different things."

"Yeah well, can't say I'm sorry you came when you did, even though I am sorry I seem to be the cause of all these new problems."

Ro Looked at me with an intense stare, "Yes who could believe that such a little slip of a thing like you could stir up so much trouble, Princess. Almost would think you had some troll in you, if I didn't know any better," Ro laughed and then looked over at Scom.

"Hey!" Scom gave an indignant cry, "All trolls are not trouble, at least not until we get caught. You know what I mean, right Princess?"

"Yeah Scom, I know exactly what you mean on that score."

After that we were all content to walk in the warm sun and let it take the morning chill out of our bones. Even Scom was quiet on our walk, taking in the sights around him as if he was trying to burn them into his memory for later reference.

After walking a few hours, the path started to climb and we soon left the sun and grass behind us. The path was now climbing into a great, wide, green forest of beautiful trees. At first the trees were crowded together and thick with underbrush. It reminded me a lot like back home. Even though the trees back home never had leaves that were purple, blood red, and black, at least not any I had seen before.

After starting into the woods, I could almost sense rather than see that there were large bodies moving along our path to each side of us. Scom must have noticed this too because he had inched closer to me for protection from our unseen stalkers. Even Mr. Blue, who had been quiet so far through our little walk, was starting to get a little agitated. The big guy kept moving his head from side to side and sniffing the air, letting out small, slight growls.

Noticing our plight, Ro looked side to side and smiled, "Don't worry, they are with us, and need to get used to strangers. By the time we get to the pass, they will be used to you all. Remember though don't wander off by yourself right now 'til they are familiar with you three." Then giving Scom an intense look, he said, "And you, troll, should especially stay within our sight. Some of the owners of that gold that went missing may take in their head to see if they could recoup their loss with a quick little bite out of your hide. If you know what I mean, troll?"

Scom paled. "Oh yes, I do know what you mean Ro," and Scom moved even closer toward my side for protection.

I was going to scold Ro for scaring the little guy and telling him that Scom was under my protection when I heard Da give a quick chuckle. Looking up into the big shape shifter's face I saw him give me a quick wink and broad smile. So I let it go, figuring that Ro was at least partially pulling the little guy's leg but I decided right there to keep a closer eye on the little troll, just in case Ro was serious.

We soon reached a small clearing where Ro had us rest from the climb to the pass. We all sat down in the open where the sun, which had been hidden from us while climbing deep in the woods, warmed our aching bodies.

As Da passed out some fruit, bread, and water to each of us, Ro looked around the clearing and seemed to decide something from the look on his face. "I think we will stay here 'til dark," he said as he walked back to our group. "I will send scouts up to the pass and I think it will be better for all of us if we cross it at night."

"You think someone or something will be there waiting for us?" I said.

"I wouldn't put it past your sister to have a few goblins or trackers up there waiting to surprise anyone foolish enough to cross the pass into her land plus I don't think the dragons will be too happy with you after what you did to Ernie," Ro said, looking up the mountain toward the pass we were aiming for. "If something is waiting for us at the pass, Princess, maybe our friends can trim down the numbers a little for us."

"So what do we do now?" I asked, stretching in the warm sun.

"Get some rest, Princess," said Da with a smile. "That's what any good solider does when he is going to war. It's lesson one of war, Princess. Eat and rest when you can for in war you can never be sure when the next time you will have a chance to do either of those will be."

I lay back with a full stomach, in the hot sun, resting up against the big, warm, furry body of Mr. Blue, figuring what the heck I'll close my eyes for a few minutes and listen to the soothing tone of the insects playing in the clearing.

"Princess, Princess, wake up, it will be time to go pretty soon," whispered a voice.

I sat up, looking around, DANG! The clearing was now in full dark and I could barely see the others moving around as they readied themselves to move out on the next part of our journey. "Whoa, how long was I out?" I said in irritation as I gathered my stuff up in the dark with the others.

"Not long, Princess," whispered Scom.

"Quiet now!" A voice out of the night, which sounded like Ro, scolded us. "The scouts we sent said there are goblins at the pass. We are going to have to sneak up on them to take them out."

"Sorry," I said, in as quiet of a voice as I could muster.

After that, the only sound was of everyone gathering all their equipment for the jaunt up the pass and our meeting with the goblins that now occupied it. Soon my eyes adjusted to the dark and I could see the outlines of my friends. Of course, it didn't help that the moon was hidden behind the clouds and there was very little light to see by.

As we gathered at the edge of the clearing, I could see what looked like Ro do a quick head count of our group. "Okay does everyone have everything they need? We're not coming back for any lost items," he said grumpily. Guess he hadn't woken up on the right side of the bed or would that be tree out here in the woods? "Now as we are going up the path just remember to follow us; no noise, and move only when we tell you to. Got it Princess?"

I nodded then realized that he couldn't see me that well and whispered, "Yeah got it."

"Scom, you got that?"

"Yeah, I got it Ro."

"Okay then let's move out quietly, and Princess stay close to your demon friend and make sure he only eats goblins. Hate to see him snack on one of our allies or a troll." With that Ro turned around and headed up the path.

I could hear Da's quiet chuckle as we started out, but even though Ro's comment miffed me a little, it did make sense to keep a close eye on the big fuzz ball anyway. Just before the trees once more enclosed me in their dark embrace, the moon peeked its face through the clouds; lighting the clearing. Looking up, I could see that it was a full moon shining brightly in the sky. Oh great, I thought, hope it isn't Friday the thirteenth too. Then I was once again stepping into the thick woods and could barely see those in front of me.

Walking slowly through the darkness, I could barely hear the whispers of movement around our little group. How these guys could move through the darkness without hitting tree branches, roots, and bushes was beyond me. Even Mr. Blue, as big as he was, moved through the woods like a ghost with no sound coming from his passage through this mess. The way I was going seemed like I hit every snag, branch, and rock there was in this woods.

As we moved up the hill toward the pass, I noticed that the trees in the woods along with the underbrush seemed to be thinning out some. In fact, the light from the full moon seemed to be shining through the trees as it peeked from behind the clouds, lighting up the darkness and making it easier to walk without tripping every few feet. After about an hour or so of climbing, Ro stopped our group for a rest. Looking around, I could see that our small group had grown to about fifty or sixty people. They were all big built men like Da. They seemed to be carrying all kinds of different weapons from huge broad swords and shields to double headed axes, and one man carrying a bag of spears or javelins on his back. The shifters looked like a motley crew of ruffians and not a proper army, but if they fought like Ro and Da, I knew that any goblins we went up against were going to have a very bad life, probably a short life at that too.

Looking around I saw Ro and Da talking to a couple of men that had just come from the direction we were headed. After talking a few minutes with a couple of other shape shifters, they walked over to where Scom and I were sitting.

"How are you doing, Princess?" whispered Ro squatting down beside us.

"I'm all right, just how much further 'til the pass?"

"Looking to fight some goblins, Princess?" chuckled Da quietly.

"Just wondering how much more walking we have to do is all."

"Well Princess, we don't have much further to go," Ro whispered. "The scouts came back and there are goblins at the pass like we thought, so we are going to take a little side path that the goblins don't know about."

"How will this help us?" I wondered aloud. "Won't we still have to hit the pass where the goblins are or will this path lead us around them?"

"No Princess, this path will bring us just above the pass, but we still have to go through where the goblins are, but coming from above them maybe we can give the goblins a little surprise they aren't expecting," said Ro, giving a nasty little laugh. I was definitely glad he was on my side of this fight. "All right let's get going and remember from here on no talking, and absolute quiet; or as quiet as you can be, Princess, while walking."

"And what's wrong with my walking?" I said with as much anger I could put in a whisper.

Ro didn't answer, but just turned away. Da laughed quietly and answered, "Princess, for a little slip of a thing that you are, you sound like a whole goblin army marching through the woods."

"Yeah okay, so I may not be an outdoorsy type of girl," I said cooling down and giving a quiet little laugh.

"Yeah, would have never guessed, Princess," Da chuckled. "Come on, let's move out, and just take it slow and watch where you put your feet, okay?"

"Yeah Da, I'll try."

"Great Princess," and with that Da reached down and pulled me to my feet.

CHAPTER 12

Our group was soon walking up the path until we hit an area where there were two large boulders leaning against each other. It looked like a small shallow cave, but I noticed that one after another of our group disappeared into its mouth. Walking in behind Da, I could see him step to the back of the cave and then step to his right where he vanished from sight.

Following in his steps, I could see what looked like a crack in the wall. Turning sideways I could slip through it with no trouble. The new path led steeply up into an enclosed area. The dark was so complete for a second or so I couldn't see my hand in front of my face. Then my eyes adjusted and I could see a small flickering light ahead, enlarging the space we were moving through. As we walked higher into the caves, more lights came up in front of us. As I came up on these lights, I could see that they were small torches set into the walls. Looking back, I could barely see the end of our line of shifters, and as the last shifter passed a torch, he put the light out.

Soon I could hear the roar of water like a large river or waterfall. Stepping out of the small cave, I could see that we had entered a large cavern. Across the cavern floor there flowed a mighty river; raging in all its white fury until it fell over a wide bottomless chasm. To cross the cavern it looked like we had to cross a narrow bridge of rock. Taking a look at the path we had to cross, I stopped and shook my head with determination.

"Oh heck no, no way am I crossing that." I know my limitations, and walking over a raging river on a bridge with no handholds had passed those limitations by a mile and then some.

Da looked at me with a smile, "Don't worry, Princess, you won't have to cross it." With that Da scooped me up and threw me over his shoulders and started over the bridge.

I don't know if I couldn't move because I was frightened or just peeved, but once we were on the bridge there was no way I was going to move and throw Da's balance off. But man, when he put me down we were going to have some very nasty words.

After watching Da walk across the path with no problems, even while carrying me, I soon started to calm down and looked at the situation with a sense of humor. Even though I was being carried like a sack of potatoes, I was getting across the bridge without killing myself or anyone else.

"Okay, Princess, I'll put you down now that we're across, but you have to promise not to be mad," Da laughed as he came to the other side of the cavern.

"It's all right, Da, just put me down now, please. This is getting a little embarrassing."

With that Da put me down on my feet with a big smile on his face. Turning around Da walked into the next cave to follow the shifters that went before us. As he did, I lit a small ball of flame in my hand and flung it at his butt.

"HEY, what the…" yelled Da.

"Oh sorry Da, hope you aren't mad," I said laughing.

Da just looked at me for a second and then laughed, "Yeah Princess, you'll do." With that he walked into the next cave with me following behind him.

We were back into what I thought was another small cave leading upward toward our goal once again; but, looking up, I could see that we were in a canyon for the rock walls stopped where a ceiling should be and above us was the night sky. I could see that the clouds had disappeared from the night and above us was the full moon and stars lighting our way toward our destination. With the light given from above, the group no longer needed torches to see where they were walking, which made for a faster trip than we had had in the darkness below.

Soon we came onto a small flat area where the first of our group sat huddling and waiting for the rest of us to catch up. As each person arrived, Ro whispered that we were to be quiet for the goblins were right over the next ridge. Since most of the group hadn't made any sounds since the start of our journey, I figured the warning was mostly aimed at Scom and me. Yeah, okay, probably mostly at me since even Scom moved through the night like a spirit making no sound.

After everyone had arrived at our new hiding place, Ro gathered us together to give us our final orders. "All right, everyone knows where to go. Remember, no goblins are to escape to warn the others." After everyone left for their positions, Ro looked at me and smiled.

"Princess, here's what I want you to do. When you see me over at that rock on the right, I want you to fire one of your fire balls into the middle of the goblins. Then I want you to duck down, that way the goblins will probably think a dragon is attacking them. Okay?"

"Yeah, okay, I can do that."

"Great I'll leave your demon protector with you, Princess.

Just stay up here after you blast the goblins."

"You know his name is Mr. Blue, right?"

"Yeah I know Princess, but I just can't call something that big and ugly Mr. Blue." With that Ro disappeared into the dark with the rest of the others.

Slowly Mr. Blue and I crept up to the edge of the ridge we were on and looked down on the goblin camp. I could see about one hundred or so goblins laying about a small rocky clearing. In the middle of the clearing, a fire crackled and sputtered to keep the goblins warm I guess, or maybe to keep the dark at bay. At each end of the clearing, where the path started there were about half a dozen goblins on guard to catch any unwary travelers crossing the pass.

Looking over at the rock Ro pointed out to me, I could see Ro waving at me. "Well here we go Mr. Blue, it's show time." Standing up, I built up a fire ball in my hands and flung it down into the middle of the goblin's fire. After picking myself up from the ground from the concussion of the explosion, I looked back down at the destruction my little flame job had caused. All that was left of the goblin's fire and any goblin within twenty feet of the fire was a smoking pit in the ground. "Oh shoot, did I do that Mr. Blue?" I guess the half growl/laugh he gave me was a yes.

Just then the other goblins seemed to be coming out of their shock and were pointing up at the ridge we were standing on. Oh yeah, too late I remembered I was supposed to be out of sight. Well, might as well take out a few more while I'm at it, so with that I flung two more balls of flame down into the middle of the two largest groups of goblins. I was about to throw a third flame down into the clearing when the shifters joined the attack.

The shifters rolled over the goblins like a wave of death.

Most goblins were slow in realizing that I wasn't the only problem they had that night and were cut down where they stood. A few goblins at the edges of the clearing tried to put up a fight, but soon succumbed to the mass of shifters that overwhelmed their numbers.

While I watched what was going on before me on the floor of the clearing, I wasn't paying much attention to the area just below me. That all changed when I heard growls, curses, and a couple sets of goblin hands appeared on the ledge I was standing on. Before I could react, I was pushed to the side by a dark mountain of fury, and the two goblins that had meant to sneak up on me were lifted into the air by two huge paws wrapped around each of their necks. Watching from the seat I had taken on the hard rock, when Mr. Blue shoved me out of the way, I saw the big fuzz ball crack the two goblin's heads together like ripe watermelons. Before I could look away, he had thrown both the goblins into the air, one at a time, and downed them in a single swallow. With a satisfied burp or two, my big friend gave me a big, fang-filled grin, and a wag of his stubby tail. Getting up off the rocks, I went over and gave the big guy a rub on his tummy. "Good job, boy, I'm so glad you are on my side," I laughed.

Looking down, I could see that none of the goblins were moving around anymore, and figured that it was all right for us to get down where everyone else was. So with a tug on one of Mr. Blue's paws, we headed down to see the damage.

Coming around the rocks that hid the path we were following, Da shouted out to me. "Hey Princess, think you could have made a bigger hole over here?" He was laughing and standing on the edge of the crater that once was the goblin fire pit. From close up it did look like I had used just a tad too much power on that shot, but what the heck, it did the trick.

About then Ro came up to me and he didn't look too happy. "You do know Princess, when I say shoot and then duck it doesn't mean for you to stand in the open and shoot fire balls, right? You do understand the concept of ducking down, right Princess?"

"Yeah well it seemed like a few more fires wouldn't hurt at the time, Ro."

"Do me a favor next time Princess, when I tell you to do something, just do it please? Think you can handle that?" And with that Ro marched away into the dark, muttering to himself about foolish princesses and taking amateurs to war.

I just stared at his retreating back until Da walked up to me chucking. "What the heck! What's his problem, Da? We got all the goblins, right?"

Da just chuckled harder, "I think he got a little close to that last fire ball you threw at the goblins and was singed, Princess. Plus I think it hurts his pride a little that you aren't as helpless as you seem, since you took out most of the goblins."

"Oh, think I should go apologize to him Da?"

"Nah Princess, just let him be. He will get over it once he gets busy again." Looking around at the destruction I had wrought, Da sighed and put his big arm around my shoulder and laughed once more, "Though I am glad you are on our side."

"Yeah, seems like everyone is having that thought tonight," I agreed, remembering having similar thoughts about my big furry buddy just a while ago on the cliffs above. Da just gave me a puzzled look. "Never mind Da, have you seen Scom anywhere?" With a shake of his head, we each parted in different directions; me to find Scom, and Da to finish his work.

CHAPTER 13

The dark shadow moved about the murky room, avoiding the little light that prevailed. "I told you, Princess Rli, that there would be a price to pay if the spell went wrong." The shadow glided over to the crumpled bundle of rags in the center of the room. "There is always a price to pay with dark magic."

Slowly the rags stood, stooped over as if the weight of the air was too much for the wretched body to hold up. "Yesss, I know, always a price for you and yours, teacher," a small whisper hissed out of the dark cloak. A small bony aged hand reached out to the shadow, as if imploring for the help it knew would never come.

The shadow stepped back in disgust from the gesture without pity or remorse. "I am sorry, Princess Rli, but my magic has its limits in this realm. You know that I have taught you more than my mistress would think was prudent. I taught you magic from the under realm, magic that no mortals are to learn, magic that belongs not of the earth, but to death."

"But I need more, teacher," the small voiced pitiful creature implored.

Slowly the shadow fades into the darkness. "No, I'm sorry Princess, but your time is at end, and I need to return to my mistress." As the voice fades, she hears a small laugh from another part of the darkness and slowly sinks to the ground, knowing that the path she has followed was truly coming to an end for her. If only I hadn't bought her back, the little brat had always been a problem was her last thoughts as exhaustion claimed her thin ravaged body.

As I sat on some rocks, I could watch, at last, the sun coming up on the small area we were camped in. Ro had us move on once it had been confirmed that all the goblins and their trackers were truly dead, and our wounded had been tended to. We had moved from the pass higher into the mountains. The place he had picked to finally camp was a familiar one, in that it was the clearing where I had met a certain dragon. Even though I know that Ernie would have sold me out, I still missed the old lizard; one silent tear of sadness leaked down my cheek.

Hearing the movement of stones under someone's feet, I wiped the tear away and turned toward my visitor. "Princess, Ro and Da would like to see you down at the fire, and I also brought you some breakfast." With a concerned look, Scom came closer. "Are you all right, Princess?"

"Yeah Scom, everything is all right, just seems like everything is coming full circle is all. Thanks for the breakfast, too by the way. Tell the guys I will be right down, okay?"

"Yes Princess, I will tell them. You know you can always talk to me, we trolls are great listeners. You know what I mean, right Princess?"

Giving the little guy a hug, I said, "Yeah I know what you mean, Scom. I can always count on you, little guy."

Looking serious, Scom took a step back and bowed,

"Thank you Princess, we trolls are not trusted easily, but you will always have this one's honor and life for all the trust you have shown me."

I couldn't help but smile at the seriousness of my little troll. "No problem, Scom, for you are my best friend in this land. Now go run and tell Ro and Da I will be right there, please." With that, Scom smiled and bowed once again and ran off to deliver my message to the others.

Sitting in the quiet left in the wake of Scom's noisy departure, I thought of all I had gone through in the little while that I had been here in this strange land; meeting creatures of lore or fairy tales like goblins, dragons, trolls, and shifters. Going from a plain, everyday girl to learning that I was a half-demon princess, and I could make one heck of a barbeque with a flick of my arm. Yes sir, this was one strange place I found myself in. Now all I had to do was find a sister that was royally peeved off at me for just being who I was and then getting rid of her so I could save my little buddy. This new place may be strange, unique and fun, but in some ways it really sucked too.

Reaching over, I thumped the ears of the sleeping big fuzz ball lying by me. With a snort and belch, the big guy rolled over and stretched out yawning showing a mouth full of teeth that would make a shark jealous.

"Some guard you are! Sleeping on the job, you big ball of fur," I kidded him as I stood to go down the hill. Mr. Blue looked so crestfallen at my rebuke that I had to laugh and hug him. "Don't worry, big guy, you're my best buddy too, and always will be number one to me." With that Mr. Blue wiggled like a small puppy and, as we moved down the path, I shared the breakfast that Scom had brought to me. Maybe, I thought, the day would be nice and quiet, but if the last few days in this world were any indication, I wasn't too hopeful about that stray thought.

After a couple of hours of sitting in the clearing, with the new gathering we had around us, I was now really sure that today wouldn't be a quiet day, as I had hoped it would be. Around one side of the clearing stood the shifters that had battled at the pass with Scom, Ro, Da, and I. Sitting across the fire was a group of goblins. These goblins were different from the goblins that were at the pass; they were a smaller version of the goblins that I had seen since I had arrived in this land.

They were there to ask our help in overthrowing my sister and their suppressors. For it seemed that my sister had recruited a group of northern goblins who, though were few in number, were much larger and fiercer then their southern cousins. With my sister's magic and the bigger goblins at her beck and call, it seems that the smaller guys were pretty much at the mercy of, what little mercy there was, of their bigger cousins in charge. Now it seems that since my sister's last visit, there had been some major changes and these guys figured we could help them get free after all this time. Seems like my sister had snapped and most of her northern friends were either dead or gone out looking for me. Looks like these guys were offering a way into the castle and a chance to change the ruler around here.

"I don't know guys, what do you think? Are these creatures on the level?" After being almost sold to the highest bidder by Ernie, I was a little leery of this gift horse, so to speak, that seemed to just drop in our lap from nowhere.

"Well Princess, before your sister came along these guys weren't saints, but they didn't cause the kind of trouble and mayhem that they do now with your sister and her friends in charge," said Ro, looking at the delegation of goblins sitting across from us. "These guys were known for their bad tempers, and a little cheating on the side, but they were always willing to trade and live with others."

Da laughed, "Not like shifters were known for their even tempers either," giving Ro a knowing look. "These guys used to be miners before your sister came here, and pretty good ones at that too. Now all she uses them for is cannon fodder for her army," Da grimaced as he kept talking. "You can't blame them for trying to break out from under your sister's control after all their problems of being used and all the lives lost."

Looking around, all I could think was that this was getting a lot more complicated every time I turned around. Seems like it was only yesterday I had nothing to worry about except waking from a dream, now I was saving some goblins, shifters, and a troll. I really needed to get back home soon before someone else was added to the list.

"Princess, Princess?"

"Yeah, umm what, Ro?"

"I said, Princess, that the goblins know a way into the castle, should we trust them?"

"Oh heck, let's go, you only live once, right?"

At that Scom sat up and whispered, "Well actually, Princess, a cat shifter is supposed to have ten lives. You know one for their human life and nine in their shifter lives. You know what I mean, right Princess?"

"Yeah Scom, I know what you're saying. Let's just hope we don't meet any cat shifters working for my sister then."

"Me personally, Princess, knowing your sister, a cat shifter would be the least of our worries," Da said with a grimace.

"Yeah I guess you're right about that, Da." Looking over at Ro, I could almost see the gears turning in the shifter's head. "Well Ro, what plan you got for us now?"

Looking up, Ro just smiled, "Plan, Princess, the only plan I have is for our new friends to get us close to your sister so we can finish her off. That's the only plan I have for us, Princess."

In the silence that followed, everyone just looked around at each other to see if something else would come from our conversation. After a moment, Da laughed out loud and slapped his knee with a thunderous sound that made everyone jump. "Well it is direct, that's for sure," laughed the big shifter. With that everyone seemed to start talking at once and the two groups, the shifters and goblins started to mix and figure out who was going where and when in storming the castle and disposing of my sister and her friends. Looked like our army had just gotten bigger by quite a bit, now let's hope that bigger also meant better too.

Later, standing with Mr. Blue by ourselves, all I could think, again, was that this little adventure was getting way out of hand and more than I had ever bargained for. Looking deep inside, I could also see that even though I knew my sister was evil, and I hardly knew her, I might not be able to get rid of her when the time came. I guess when you grow up not know who your real family is, any port in the storm would do, even a port that isn't so great. Back home I had a great foster mother and father and their daughter waiting for me, but this was my own flesh and blood I was going up against.

"Princess?" whispered a voice from behind us.

Turning around I saw my three friends who had started out from the valley with me along with two small goblins. The five of them were looking at me as if they didn't want to disturb my quiet time, but they had urgent things to discuss. Well, of course, half the goblin's attention also seemed to be on my big fuzzy buddy standing next to me too. Guess his reputation of having goblins as snacks preceded him. Putting my hand on his furry belly and giving him a rub, I asked my friends, "Okay, what's up guys?"

Ro stepped forward. "Princess, these two goblins are the leaders of the rebels and want to meet you since they have heard so much of your power."

"Oh hi guys, nice to meet you." Both goblins bowed low, without coming any closer. I wasn't sure if it was me or Mr. Blue, but I was betting it was the big fuzz ball next to me they were really afraid of. As they stood up, I stepped forward to talk to them when both goblins hopped back with a look of fright in their beady little eyes. Well maybe it wasn't my furry friend they were mostly afraid of after all.

Taking a step back, I said in a low voice so not to frighten our new friends, "We are friends now and we will not hurt you. We're here to help."

One of the goblins stepped forward. "It is just that you look like your sister when she first came to us, Princess."

"Oh well, thanks, I guess?"

"We have listened to the shifters and they say you are not your sister, that you are good, not evil. We came to see if that is true for ourselves, Princess. Our people have to know the truth, since we have been lied to most of our lives."

"I'll tell you guys, am I some savior or angel? No, I don't think so and don't really want to be either. Am I some gal that got thrust into a situation and is trying to do her best with it? Yes. All I can say is that I'm not my sister and that should count for something, right?"

I just stood there as each of the goblins looked me in

the eyes. They say the eyes are the window to the soul, if that's true then the goblins must have liked how my soul looked for they soon relaxed and once again bowed.

"You're right, Princess, as you say you are not your sister, and that is all we can really ask for," said the first goblin and with that both goblins bowed low and then headed back down the path to the swelling armed camp below.

Da looked after the goblins, shaking his head with a look of wonder on his face. "Well that's a first, a goblin taking someone's word for fact without arguing. You do constantly surprise me, Princess."

"That's okay Da, I'm constantly surprising myself too in this place," I said with a small sad smile. "Now let's see if we can go surprise my sister and get this whole adventure over with. What do you think, guys, shall we get this circus on the road?"

As my four friends followed me down the path, I heard Da ask no one in particular, "What is a circus?"

Another voice whispered behind my back, "And why is it going on the same road as us? You know what I mean?"

Smiling and giving a little chuckle, I gave Mr. Blue a pat on the arm. Who knows, maybe we could surprise my sister, she would come to her senses, and nobody would get hurt. As my smile faded, the thought flashed in my head that I couldn't be that lucky. Never was, never will. Oh well, a girl can wish.

As we gathered with the small army around us, Ro and Da came up with sly grins on their faces. "Okay, what is it now?" I asked.

Da laughed as he clapped Ro on the shoulders, "Well, Princess, while you were off thinking my brother here came up with a plan after all."

"Well, great what's the plan, if I may ask?"

Ro looked at me like I was going to bite and seemed to have wanted to step back from me except for Da's hands on his shoulders holding him in place. "The plan is that I will go with some of the goblins and shifters through a tunnel that they told us about. You and Da and the rest of the group will head for the castle's front gate."

"Okay go on," I prodded.

"Okay well, the tunnel will lead us to the front gate and then we open it to let the rest of you through and then we take care of your sister, so that's the whole plan, Princess." Ro looked slyly over at me.

"Nice plan Ro, just one little change." Looking over Ro's shoulders, I could see Da chuckling and Ro's shoulders cringing. But I wanted to make sure that I would be where the main action was.

"And that change is, Princess?" Ro said quietly while Da's laughter grew louder and was now joined by other shifters and goblins.

"The change is that I'm going with you." As I stepped closer to Ro, he cringed more as Da laughed harder and small sparks of flames leaped from my finger tips. "And there is nothing you can say to change my mind, got me shifter?"

"Yes Princess," whispered Ro as he shook Da's hands off his shoulders and he stomped away from me with a gale of shifter and goblin laughter following in the wake of his departure.

About an hour later we all took off, heading for the point where the two groups would split, each headed toward their final destination and the assault on my sister's home base.

CHAPTER 14

Jax stood outside the two doors that led to his mistress' room, wondering if the next few seconds would be his last on this world – for his mistress did not reward bad news with kindness. Standing there, Jax thought about how he had gotten in this mess, and even if he made it back to the barracks would the last of the Princess' guards he was in charge of still be there. Jax had a sneaking suspicion that the guards were ready to steal back home to the north instead of dying for some half-crazed princess here in the south.

Just as Jax was stepping forward, the doors burst open as if a wild fury was trying to escape from the room; it slammed the heavy slabs of stone aside like paper, cracking the walls on each side of the entrance.

"Come in, my general," whispered a voice from the dark.

"Princess, I come with some bad news," Jax said in a voice that trembled in fear.

"Don't bother, general, I know the news and it is of no importance to me anymore." The voice in the dark raised in pitch, making the large goblin quake in his boots even more than before, expecting his life to end any second in some very unpleasant and spectacular fashion. "Go and take what pitiful excuses for warriors that you have left and leave me. I have learned more dark secrets from my books than what my teacher has taught me, I will have a real army when I need it."

Jax stood there hardly believing his luck when the voice sounded once again, "GO NOW, BEFORE I KILL YOU ALL!" The voice now echoed and bounced off the walls in the hall, breaking the trance that Jax seemed to be in and making him move faster than he ever had in his life. As he ran toward the barracks to gather his men, the heavy doors slammed shut causing cracks in the doors with dirt and dust falling from the ceiling. Jax thought maybe his men had the right idea about heading back home to the north.

Now that we had arrived at the point where the two groups were to go their separate ways, it seemed that I had two problems – one small size problem and one large size problem and no idea how to deal with either one. "I'm sorry, Mr. Blue, but you can't come with me. The goblins have told us that the tunnels are too small for you in some places, and I want to go with the tunnel group." Also, I thought, having the big guy in a small tunnel with a bunch of goblin snacks would not be a good idea.

Mr. Blue just looked at me with those big, sad eyes that a little puppy gets when you use a harsh voice. "Oh don't do that, you just can't come. Now you be a good fuzz ball and go with Da, and then you will have a lot of big northern goblins to munch when we attack, okay big guy?"

Mentioning the chance for northern goblin snacks seemed to pacify the big guy somewhat even though I noticed that all the goblins close enough to hear seemed to be stepping back from my big, fuzzy protector. Well that seems to have taken care of the big size problem, now for the small size problem.

Turning away from Mr. Blue, I looked down at Scom. Before I could say a word, Scom spoke up, "I'm not too small for the tunnels, Princess, and my place is at your side. You know what I mean, right, Princess?"

"Yes I do Scom; I do know what you mean," I said quietly as I bent down to talk to the little guy on his level. "But I need you for something important for me, Scom, that only you can do."

"What is that, Princess?"

"I need you to be my eyes and ears with Da's group, Scom. You are the only one I can trust, you know. Plus, I thought, it would keep you out of danger (as much as possible). Come on, you don't think I would leave such important work like sneaking up on my sister's castle to mere goblins and shifters, do you? This job calls for the talent of a great troll like you, Scom."Looking over the little guy's head, I could see both Ro and Da smiling and nodding as I talked to Scom.

"Oh you are so right, Princess, only a troll is really good at sneaking around castles."

The little guy looked so earnest with the new job assigned him that I couldn't help but smile and give him a hug, hoping that I was doing the right thing in sending him with Da; after all, it was just a small tunnel we were going in. What could happen, right? As this thought flashed into my head, I felt a small shiver run down my back. Yeah, hope that thought doesn't put a jinx on things.

Ro, looking on, nodded his head at me, "Time to go, Princess. We want to be off the mountain paths and in the tunnels before daylight."

"Okay Ro." Giving Scom and Mr. Blue a hug each, I went over to Da and the two goblins that seemed to be in charge of the group going with him. "Watch them both,

Da." I whispered as I hugged the large shifter.

"Always for you, Princess," Da said giving me a big squeeze back.

Stepping back and looking at the goblins standing by Da, with a glare, I warned them. "If you cause anything to happen to my friends you will wish, for the remainder of your very short lives, that you had never met me. We do understand each other, right?"

Both goblins stepped back nodding and gulping with what I took as understanding. Shifting my gaze to the other goblins and the shifters in this group to include them all, I added in a stern voice. "That's good because there is nowhere in this world you could hide from me, if even a hair is harmed on my friend's heads, understand." By now even the other goblins from the group were nodding and most had lost what green color they had and were white from fright. The shifters on the other hand, looked at me with a new level of respect and shock on their faces. "Well okay then, let's go," I said with a smile turning and heading up the path leading to the tunnels.

Behind me I could hear the goblins and shifters going with me scrambling to catch up. Over that I also could hear Da laughing and urging on the goblins and shifters I had just left, to head to the path that they would need to take to get to the castle gate.

Walking quickly but quietly, our group moved up the mountain path that the goblins said would take us to the tunnel's entrance. It wasn't a difficult climb and soon the small path headed down into a rock strewn valley. Just before dawn, we came to a halt before a small dark cave entrance hidden behind two boulders.

"This is where we go in," whispered one of the goblins.

"We must be quiet for we don't want to wake them, oh and we will need light."

"Who are them?" I whispered to Ro as he helped the goblins light torches that had been bought along for the trip.

"You're okay with bugs, right Princess?" Ro questioned with a peculiar look on his face.

"What kind of bugs are we talking about, Ro?" I noticed that my voice was rising and tried to bring it back down to a whisper again.

"Well Princess, it's not so much the kind of bugs as how big these particular bugs might be." By now the torches had been lit and the first of our group was ready to enter the tunnel.

"Oh shoot, I really, really hate bugs – almost as much as I hate heights," I muttered under my breath.

"What was that, Princess?" asked Ro with a concerned look on his face.

"Nothing, let's just get this little hike over with, shall we?" I added in a louder and, I hope, more confident voice, and with that the first of the group headed into the tunnel entrance. As we entered, the darkness of the tunnel covered us in its inky blackness. Even the rising dawn's light and the feeble flickering torches could not penetrate far into the dark,

"Princess, if you could give us a little more light?" a voice whispered from the dark.

"Right, no problem guys, one sec." Holding my hand up in front of me, a small glow lit up chasing back the blackness of the tunnel.

"Thanks," Ro said. "Now that we can see better, let's move out."

For the first part of our trek, the tunnel was dry and narrow and I could see by the feeble light that Mr. Blue and most of the shifters like Da would have had a hard time getting through this area. I also noticed, as we traveled, that the tunnel seemed to head at a downward angle from the cave mouth and I hoped that the goblins knew where they were going, for there was hardly any room to turn around if we needed to.

The tunnel's ceiling was so low that the top of my wings were rubbing on the rough stone, and that Ro and the other shifters could not stand up to their full height as we walked along. I guess being short had its advantages sometimes, you know, like in scary small holes in the ground.

Moving under the ground with only the hint of light from my hand, the feeble, sputtering torches and with no sky above, I soon lost track of time. I couldn't tell if we had been walking for minutes, hours or days, but I could tell that the path we had been following was leveling out and ahead I caught glimpses of a bright light shining out of a hole in the tunnel ahead.

As it came my turn to step out of the tunnel, I could see that we were all standing on a slab of rock perched high above a flowing mass of light and intense heat below us. As I looked down, I snuffed out the flame in my hand for the river of lava below us lit up the cave with its brilliance.

As the others in the group gathered around, I saw that there was a bridge across the flowing pool of lava that led to another cave entrance. Of course, I thought, none of these places could have an escalator across; they all have to have these little walkways without rails, don't they? Man, I hate heights!

Half listening to Ro and the goblin leaders discuss the best way across, I felt a growing pull inside of me. I wanted nothing more than to step out on that bridge and to dive into the flowing inferno below me and to drink in its warmth and light. Slowly I could feel my feet take me closer to the edge of the walkway, as in a dream. By my side, the small knife I carried opposite my ice sword vibrated and gave off a glow that shone through the edges of its sheath.

"Princess, where do you think you are going?" I could hear Ro ask as from a distance. I just kept walking and as my feet hit the beginning of the crossing, I could see flames flicker up from the pool below, reaching and searching in hunger. As I stepped out further, I felt myself pull the knife and hold it at my side, then I crossed a barrier not seen by the others but felt by me.

All sounds of our group disappeared from behind me and it was as if I was alone in this world of heat and light and the crackle of flames. My steps soon bought me to the center of the bridge where I stopped, feeling in my bones that I was at the apex of some unseen power. Around me the flames grew higher, reaching to the top of the cave. Below me I could see the inferno stir and swirl in violent circles, sending spurts of liquid fire up into the air.

As more flames and liquid seemed to fill the air, I could feel my hand raise the knife in front of my face. As I looked at the shining metal, it glowed as bright as a red star in the skies. From all around me, the flames in the air jumped at the edges and point of my knife and with each strike, I could feel it grow heavier in my hand. The knife was soon as long as the ice sword that hung at my side. The two swords, the one that I wore at my side and the one I now held in my hand, warred against each other – one trying to chill the heat in my body and the other trying to dampen the cold.

As more power entered the sword, I could soon feel it flowing down into my body, filling me with its power as it had done with the weapon in my hand. After what seemed like a lifetime, the last of the light and heat was gone and all felt silent and dark.

"PRINCESS, PRINCESS, WHERE ARE YOU?" Through the darkness, I could hear what sounded like Ro shouting my name along with the other voices of the shifters in either fright or anger, maybe a little bit of both.

Lighting a small flame in my hand once again, I could see my small group of adventurers walking toward me with looks of wonder on their faces. "What's up, guys?" I asked, my voice sounding to me as if I had awakened from a long sleep.

"Are you hurt, Princess?" Ro asked with a look of concern on his normally rock steady face.

"Sure, I'm fine, but we probably should move off this bridge. I don't think it's a good idea to talk over a pit of fire, do you guys?"

"Uhh Princess, look down. What fire?" Ro asked as he pointed downward.

Looking down was like coming fully awake from a dream, for I could see that what had been a pool of lava a couple of minutes ago was nothing but solid rock below us. "Oh did I do that? So that's why the lights went out, just thought you guys forgot to pay the electric bill." Everyone just stood there with a look of concentration on their face, as if they were trying to figure out what I was talking about. "Never mind guys, let's just get to the other side, okay?"

With that we moved to the opposite side of the bridge. No one said another word to me until everyone was over and ready to move on. Then, of course, Ro was the first to speak. "Princess, I think that we need to rest and see that you are okay."

"I just need to put away this sword and I'll be ready to

go." Looking down I could see that the small sheath that had held the fire sword as a knife had grown as the sword had grown. Wow, guess some of this magic stuff was pretty cool after all, I thought. Putting the sword away and standing up, I could see that it was now hard to turn around without hitting something with one sword or the other. Well, this is going to be a pain. It's not as if I wasn't clumsy enough without adding two swords to the mixture.

"Here let me fix that, Princess," said Ro as he unbuckled the belts around my hips and strapped them across my chest and back. "If you do this right, it shouldn't interfere with your wings and your swords will be easier to draw from this position. There now, how's that?"

Reaching behind me, I drew the swords, as I had seen done in countless movies. "Yeah that will work," I said as I then checked for freedom of movement to fly. As I lifted off the ground a few feet, I thought fleetingly of the power I was gaining in this land and hoping that it wasn't as corrupting to me as it seemed to have been to my sister.

Looking down on the goblins and shifters below me, I now saw looks again of wonder mixed in with trust and the willingness to follow me into battle. Even in Ro's eyes I could see a new look of respect and determination. Hopefully my actions would justify all the trust I saw before me.

Coming back down to the ground, I sheathed both my swords. I could feel the heat and iciness radiating from each sword as their individual powers clashed against each other. "We should get going now, don't you think Ro? I mean we have spent so much time on the bridge with the fire sword that I don't think we should waste anymore."

Everyone looked at me, puzzled. "What do you mean, Princess? You were only on the bridge for a minute or two, and then the flames went out." Ro said with a look of concern.

"Oh," I squeaked, "guess it seemed longer on my end of things than on yours. Never mind, I'm fine and I don't think we should wait anymore, okay."

One of the goblins stepped forward and bowed low saying, "As you wish, Princess, but we are entering their area now and I think it wise if we had more light."

"And what are these things that we need light to keep away from us, pray tell?"

"Very wicked things," said the goblin turning a faint shade of his green color and backing up so that he was standing once again within the group of his fellow goblins, "very wicked, nasty, crawly things indeed, Princess."

Looking at the rest of the group, I could see that everyone was a little hesitant to move on, but if we were to meet up with the others we needed to march out of here soon. "Well, I can only give so much light guys, so what are we going to do now?" I said.

"Don't worry, Princess," Ro stepped from the crowd. "We have a few bigger torches saved for this part of the trip. We will just need you to light them for us, please."

"Oh well, yeah I can do that. Thought for a second it was something hard you wanted me to do there, guys." So with a quick little touch to each of the torches, we had the cave lit up almost like daylight had come to the darkness and everyone seemed to breathe a little easier as we walked into the next part of the tunnel we were traversing.

As we moved out on our path, I saw that this tunnel was wider than the last we had been in. Four bodies could move side by side down this wide avenue. Looking up at the round smooth ceiling and the sides of the wall, I could see that our lights reflected off of them as if they were made of glass."Uhm, Ro?"

"Yes, Princess," Ro answered with an air of distraction.

"Just exactly what made this part of the tunnel?"

"Princess, remember when I asked you how you felt about bugs?"

"Well yes," then it hit me what Ro was trying to say. "Oh crap, I thought you meant little bugs, not something big enough to make this place," I said, my voice rising a little in what I wasn't certain was either anger or concern.

"It will be okay, Princess, as long as we are quiet and don't raise our voices," Ro said, as he gave me a frown.

"Yeah, sorry Ro," I whispered back as he gave me a smile with my apologies.

For what seemed like a long time, we followed the glass tunnel until it started to turn up toward the surface. Ro stopped us at the point where the tunnel turned upward and gathered us together to give us all further instructions. Looking up, I could see that the glass tunnel ended just above us and went back to good old solid rock again. "Okay, I think we are pretty much safe now. The tunnel above us leads to the front gate. When we get to the gate, we let in our friends on the outside and take the castle. Any questions?" No one answered since we had all been through this briefing before. "Okay, so let's head out."

Just as Ro stepped toward the path leading up, the glass wall just behind me disappeared and I caught a fleeting glance of something big striking the goblin next to me holding a torch. Soon we were in total blackness, filled with the sounds of screams, weapons striking hard bodies, and the sound of meat being ripped apart.

Freezing for a second, I tried to sort through all the sounds of the battle in the dark hole we found ourselves in. Then it clicked, oh yeah, light. Reaching back, I drew out both of my swords and the tunnel was lit by two separate but distinctive lights, one hot and red, the other cold and blue.

Looking at the scene lit up before me, I could see goblin and shifter bodies down all around us; granted it wasn't as bad as it sounded in the dark, but it wasn't good either. A hissing sound to my front brought me back to the fight. In front of me was what looked like a giant cockroach. This guy was a little too big for me to step on, and there was no can of bug spray handy. He was about four feet long and we were looking eye to eye. The pinchers that clicked in front of its mouth looked razor sharp, and from the condition of the bodies I had seen around us, this guy knew how to use them with deadly efficiency.

As he got closer, seeing the others trying to fight off the bugs around us, as still more seemed to pour from tunnels in the wall, I felt a red hot burning anger that seemed to make each sword in my hand blaze even more. The creature before me stopped and hissed at the bright light. "WELL, I DON'T HAVE A CAN OF RAID, BUT LET'S SEE IF THESE WILL DO!" I yelled as I twirled each sword, cutting through the bug in front of me like a hot knife through butter.

Rushing down the tunnel floor, I could hear someone screaming as in a war cry, but couldn't make out the words. Then it clicked in that it was me making that sound, and that I was soon standing in the middle of the tunnel surrounded by bug parts and guts. The bugs were gone and about half our group was still standing, though most showed signs of our recent battle.

Ro came through the crowd, looking around at the pile of body parts at my feet. "You know, Princess, remind me never to get you mad at me, okay?" All around the others gave me wary smiles.

"Yeah, no problem, Ro," I said as I sheathed my two swords. "Now let's boogie before those things come back." Everyone just looked at me with a blank stare. "Never mind, guess disco didn't make it here. Let's go, guys." With that we reluctantly left our dead behind and climbed the path leading us up to the castle gate and, hopefully, to the end of my sister.

CHAPTER 15

She sat huddled in the middle of her throne, watching a glowing globe that she held tightly in her hands. She watched as the group underground was attacked by her friends from the hive. The queen had promised that this group would be wiped out. Then just as she thought all would be destroyed, her sister once again came through and fought off the hive's queen and her guards. With a scream and grimace, she tossed the globe to the ground where it shattered into a hundred different pieces.

Could no one follow orders and rid her of her baby sister? How could someone have such luck? It was almost as if she had the nine lives of a cat. The buzzing of insects brought her attention back to the room around her. As she looked at the annoying insects buzzing around what was left of her two pets, the noise drilled through her brain. She wondered how her pets had been killed. Had her sister already been down here; killing her best friends, her lovely pets? No, deep down a voice in her head answered. A fleeting image of mad laughter and the last, agonized cries of her pets echoed through her mind. Images of their gory death were fighting to the surface of her crazed brain.

No, no it was her sister, all her fault. I will fix her, yes I will, she thought as she reached for an old book sitting on the arm of the throne. Looking down at the page, she hissed an evil laugh that grew as the light of sanity once again left her eyes. "Yes, the dead will not fail, not like all the others," she whispered quietly, her voice barely registering above the constant buzz of the insects around the throne.

The tunnel we followed led us to a stone wall where we halted to rest. The trip, while short, had been fraught with tension with the thought that we might be attacked once again, even though we were out of the bug's home. Now that we were almost at the end of our journey, everyone breathed a sigh of relief. I guess everyone figured that fighting what was in the castle couldn't be as bad as the bugs. I had some thoughts about that, but kept them to myself, not wanting to stir everyone's fears up again.

After a couple of minutes, everyone prepared themselves for what was lurking behind the wall we were facing. Slowly one of the goblins opened the hidden door and one by one we all filed through the opening. As the last of us entered the room, the wall closed; shutting out the fear of the bugs that seemed to be lurking just behind us.

Looking around, I could see that we were in a two story, round room. The room had steps that wound around the outer wall and led up to a platform. Along the platform wall there were small openings or windows every few feet. I could see that the platform ran into an opening in the wall. Some of the goblins and shifters had climbed the stairs and disappeared into the opening I had just noticed.

Ro came up to me and seeing where I was looking, explained, "That platform leads across the top of the gate and into the other gate house, Princess."

"And what are those windows above the platform for?"

"Those are for the defenders to protect the gate. From those windows, they can rain down arrows or anything else that takes their fancy. Makes it hard to take this castle, that's one of the reasons it's never been tried before, Princess."

"Seems funny that there isn't anyone here guarding the gate," I observed.

Before Ro could answer, one of the shifters that had gone through the opening above us whistled and waved to catch Ro's attention. As he left to find out what was up, I continued to look around the room we had entered. I could see that besides the stairs and platform there was a large set of gears with a heavy chain wrapped around it. I figured that this was what lowered and raised the gate of the castle. I also noticed some goblins standing before a small door leading to what I figured were the castle's inner areas as they seemed to be listening carefully for any sound that our small group had been discovered.

I noticed that Ro was done with whatever important information was being passed on to him and he was gathering the shifters around him. Wandering over, I glanced at the windows again and saw that it was light out, but that it was a subdued light filtering through the openings. Must be close to dawn, I thought.

As I walked up to the gathered group, I could hear Ro making plans. "The other gate house is ours," he said "At full dark we will open the gates and . . ."

"What? We have to wait a full day here, what if someone comes along and finds us?" I questioned with a voice of concern.

"Princess, it will be dark in an hour, that's the sunset you see from the windows. We were down in the tunnels for a full day."

"Oh, sorry, go on," I whispered as I felt the heat of

embarrassment creep up my face.

Ro just gave me a tolerant smile and continued. "Anyway, once we are all in the castle, we head for the main keep and then find your sister, Princess, where we take care of her. Any questions, anyone?"

"Yeah, just one little question, Ro," I said looking around at the gate room. "Not that I'm complaining after our little dance with the bugs, but where are my sister's soldiers? I just don't see her giving everyone a day off, you know?"

Ro and most of the group looked around with concern and worry too. "Yeah, I do know what you mean, Princess, but I'm not going to go look for trouble before we have to. If there are no guards here, so be it; just makes it easier for us in the long run," Ro said, and with that everyone drifted off to their assigned area to wait 'til darkness and the coming attack; each alone with their thoughts.

———————————

As darkness slowly gathered in the room we were in, Ro allowed small lights to be lit to chase the shadows back; giving some small comfort to those waiting to go to war. As brave as the gathered shifters and goblins were, the small lights helped everyone to forget the dark tunnels and the creatures that lived in them. I could tell that our entire group would rather take the chance of discovery by those that dwelled in the castle than to sit in the gathering darkness.

Sitting there, waiting, my mind once again drifted to my older sister and I wondered why she had brought me back to this land. If she had left me in the world I knew, none of this would be happening. I just hoped that when this whole thing was done, I could go home. Of course, with the way my luck has been running, my other sisters would turn out to be as crazy as this one and I'd have to fight all three of them before I got home, I thought with a slight shiver.

I was roused out of my dark thoughts of the coming family reunion by the movement of the others as they got ready for the attack. As the small door leading into the castle was opened, I could hear the gears of the gate slowly moving, lowering it to let our friends into the castle.

The door we went out led into the castle courtyard. As I entered the open area, I saw our group spread out to fight any that opposed us. Looking around I could see, as all of us could, that this area was as empty as the last. This was wrong, very wrong. We should have met someone by now. I had a very bad feeling about this.

Hearing a roar behind us, I turned to face our enemies at last only to see that it was Da's group entering the castle through the now fully open gate. The roar had been Mr. Blue as he had spotted me in the group standing in the courtyard. As he rushed toward me, I could see the stub of his tail wagging and in his haste he bowled over several shifters and goblins. "Yo, big fellow, slow down," I said as he got closer, but the sound of my voice only seemed to spur him on more. With another roar, he scooped me up in his arms and hugged me.

Trying not to breath in the aroma, of what smelled like old wet dog, I patted the big fuzz ball on the arms and chest and tried to get him to put me back down. Note to myself, when we were done with this battle – the big guy needed a bath.

After a few more seconds, Mr. Blue finally put me down and Ro, Da, and some of the goblins came over to where we were standing. "Well, Princess, if your protector yelling doesn't bring out the bad guys, I would say that no one is home," Ro said as he patted Mr. Blue on the back.

"I think you're right, Ro. I think the goblins are gone,

but I feel that my sister is still around here somewhere, just waiting for us." Looking around the group, I spotted Scom and gave him a smile. "Nice to see you made it, little guy."

He smiled back and said "Yes, Princess, and nice to see you again. If you know what I mean?"

"Well Ro, now what do we do since it seems we're throwing a party and no one wants to come?" I asked, looking around at the deserted grounds.

"We take the main part of the castle and search for your sister, Princess," Ro answered with a smile.

With that we moved through the castle. Looking up, I could see that this part of the castle was only about three stories high. Not nearly as impressive as I thought it would be. Nearing the large double doors of the keep, I could see that they were partially open. Still fearing a trap, we entered the doors and into a small round chamber. In the chamber there was a high ceiling that went to the top of the keep, the only other thing inside was a large hole in the middle of the floor that had what looked like steps leading down into its depths. Ro and I looked at each other with concern when one of the goblins stepped up to us and bowed. "Your sister's throne room is down there, Princess," he said pointing at the hole in the floor.

"Of course it is," I said with a resigned sigh. "Where else could it be but underground?" Looking around, I could tell that I wasn't the only one in the group that wasn't happy with the present situation.

CHAPTER 16

"Well, might as well as get the show on the road so to speak. Let's go, guys," I said as I walked toward the entrance of my sister's throne room, in what I hoped was a brave voice. Going down those stairs wasn't that bad, it was well lit by torches on each landing and wide enough for two people to walk side by side down the flat, smooth, stone steps. The stairs wound around and around the floor opening and came out into a large chamber at the bottom. Across the chamber were two huge, cracked doors. These doors were set into the walls on each side, and looked, at one time, to be solid thick stone, but were now bound together by iron bands. I could feel in my bones that my sister was waiting on the other side of those doors, I was just a little worried about what else was waiting with her to greet us.

As we approached the doors, I could hear muttering and questions behind me wondering how we were to get through the barrier in front of us but, as we got closer, I could see that the doors were slightly ajar and it soon fell silent behind me.

Ro gestured for a couple of the biggest shifters to open the doors before us. As they moved the massive slabs of stone open, I could see how heavy it was by the way that

the arm and leg muscles bulged on the shifters and the
effort they put in moving the weight of the doors.

Moving into a cavernous open area, I could see at the
far end a small, thin figure sitting up on the only seat in the
room. It seemed to be rocking back and forth and was
muttering words to itself. We all stopped just inside the
room in shock, but it wasn't the sight as much as the smell
that froze our feet. The smell was as of a long decayed
grave opened, or a festering wound left open to drain out
its venomous sludge. It was as if the smell had a physical
feel to it, a wall that stopped us all in our tracks.

We could not see what was causing the smell because
the room was dark and only a few flickering lights lit the
lone figure and chased the shadows of the night away.
"Hello my sssister," came a hissing sound from the figure
sitting on the throne. "I sssee you have brought friendsss."

"Yes I have, sister," I said as I moved toward the small
figure, trying to pierce the dark flickering shadows to get a
better glimpse of her; but between the dark and the robes
hiding her, I couldn't discern anything about the figure
speaking. So I moved closer, walking up the steps toward
the mysterious figure that I was hoping was my sister.

"We have come here to fight you if we must, but I
would like to talk out whatever problems there are between
us, Rli."

"NO!" she shouted as she rose from her seat. "My little
sssister, I know why you are here, you wish to sssteal my
power as you did before we ssent you to that other world."
As she spoke, a slim, slimy bony hand poked out of her
robe, and I caught a glimpse of her withered body beneath
her coverings. It looked like whatever spells she had used in
the valley had backfired on her big time and she was paying
for it with the decimation of her body.

"You're wrong, Rli. I really don't want your power; I

just want a family that I didn't even know I had. Anyway you're the one that brought me back here. If you were afraid that I was going to take your powers why not just leave me where I was?" I asked as I topped the steps to Rli's throne.

"My teacher, my tutor – or was it that voice I heard – sssaid I needed to bring you back to get rid of you. That you were plotting against all of usss, the three of us, to ssteal our powers as you almost did our mother's."

"But Rli, she lied because until a few days ago, I didn't even know that I had sisters or a mother."

"The voices I hear have no reason to lie to me," Rli whispered as she slowly sank back to her seat. "Ssshe promised me, I would never lose my power to one ssuch as you, like our mother did."

Looking at the pitiful thing sitting before me, all I could think of was getting my hands onto the throat of Rli's teacher. Seems like my mother wasn't all that hot in picking tutors that didn't stab their students in the back, and speaking of my mother, I asked, "What do you mean I stole our mother's powers, Rli?"

She looked up at me slowly and gave a little laugh. "You're half demon, our mother was a witch, and the combination produces you, someone who with her bare touch would suck the power or magic right out usss."

Thinking back over the last couple of days, I thought that Rli must be wrong for I had touched and brushed up against trolls, goblins, and shifters and had no adverse effect on them and said as much to her.

"No, you wouldn't affect them, their power is natural not magic in this world. You can only steal the magic or life force that controls it."

"But how can I do that?" I asked in awe.

"No one knows," Rli whispered. "When our mother

had you, each month that you were inside her you leached power out of her, she barely made it to your birth alive. Then, after you were born, every touch sucked the power from each of us. As you grew, so did your ability to take more of our magic."

"Oh," I whispered as I sat down on the top step, "that's why you sent me away?"

Rli laughed, "Of course that's why. Mother was so weak by this time we first banished her for punishment for even having you. Then it was your turn; we sent you away to someplace with no magic at all, a world of metal and technology, a place where we send all outcasts and thieves."

Standing up, I looked down on the pathetic creature that sat before me, knowing that even though we were of the same blood, I could no longer count her as family. "All you guys had to do was leave me on my own, I mean I didn't steal on purpose, I'm not that kind of person."

Rli looked up once again from her seat, her eyes dark and foreboding in the flickering light. "Oh, but you would have stolen what was not yours to have, little sister. You have our mother's blood, our blood, and no good comes from the blood that flows though your body."

Looking down at the bottom of the steps, I could see the group of goblins and shifters that had been listening to our little conversation as they moved closer to us, the look of concern on their faces made my heart sink. I wasn't like my family, no matter whose blood flowed through my veins, hadn't I proved that through helping at the mountain pass and in the tunnels. Turning back to my sister, I looked her in the eyes and whispered, "You're wrong, Rli, I'm not like you and my friends are proof that I'm good."

"Well dear sister, in that case I guess I need to get rid of these so called friends of yours then," Rli said as she rose up once again out of her seat, laughing and waving her arms across the throne room. As she did this, the ground under our feet started to tremble and small dimples in the throne room floor appeared every few feet.

"Oh heck, now what have you done?" I said looking between my sisters' crazed eyes and the action on the temple floor.

"Why jussst a little trick, my sister, that my tutor ssshould have taught me."

CHAPTER 17

She sat in her throne in deep thought, staring at the bright fire roaring in the hearth, but not really seeing the flames dancing within. She felt a pull, a deviation in her world as if a change was blowing in the wind, that is if the under realm had had a wind blowing within it. Around her, spirits of the dead roamed, going about their tasks to serve the Mistress of the realm. "Where is she?" the figure whispered, looking up and around her yet knowing that none of those moving about could answer her question.

She catches the sound of moving feet within the silent hallways approaching her room. Entering, a robed figure bows low and approaches, shying away from the light of the fire. "My Mistress, I came as soon as you called. I . . ."

"Teacher, why does Rli call the dead?" she asks, cutting off her servant's greetings and getting right to the point of what is brothering her this day. "I hold you responsible for this mess."

Slowly the robed figure stands and looks at her, "I never taught her this magic, my Mistress, I . . ."

"And yet she is now calling those that are mine to command up from my realm to fight her petty little human war," she whispers, her voice dropping even lower in tone (a very dangerous tone), as the teacher knows from past experience with her mistress.

The teacher bends down, hiding in her robes. Knowing that now is not the time to anger her mistress, if she doesn't want to end up like the other shadows roving around the realm; slim slivers of their former selves with no free will, floating about and existing only to serve their mistress in her world.

"Take care of this, teacher, for there are others that can take your place. Bring the one that stole mine to me," and with that she sits back once again in her chair and stares into the fire, dismissing from her thoughts the shadow slowly rising from the floor and slinking toward the door.

"Oh I'll take care of her, I'll take care of both of them; then I'll take care of you, my mistress," the teacher whispers as she moves and glides back into the shadows, back to her student's castle.

Looking down at the floor of Rli's throne room, I can see bodies rising up through the dimples in the floor. As they move toward the group of goblins and shifters below us, the group gathers closer together and starts inching up the steps toward my sister and me. Looking over at Rli again I asked in a louder voice, "What are those things?"

My voice seems to penetrate her insanity for a second and she once again focuses on my face. "Why, my little sister, these are the undead from the under realm, they are mine now to command, to destroy you and your friends."

Looking down at the group gathering before us at the bottom of the stairs and then back at my sister, I squeaked out, "You mean you conjured up zombies to fight us?"

All movement stopped in the hall, everyone in the hall, including my sister, looked at me with a questioning look. "What the heck are zombies?" she asked.

"You know zombies, the undead, kill, rip apart, and eat people, suck the brains out of people's heads for dinner, you know zombies," I said looking all around me, noticing that some of those around us were staring at me like I had grown another head and some were turning shades of green, even some of the undead looked a little paler than before.

Rli just stared at me for a second and then in a shocked voice said, "That's just disgusting, sister. What kind of place did we send you to? These are undead warriors to fight your friends. Ugh, who would eat someone's brains? That is just sick."

So okay, I guess zombie movies haven't made it here either. As this thought passed through my head, the undead started to move once again against my friends, backing them ever upwards as they gathered closer to me to form a protective circle around the top of the throne steps.

As her army moved up to meet my friends, I could hear my sister muttering strange words under her breath, then watching my friends once again I saw the first of the undead go down under the weapons of those in the front of the line. Well this is going better than expected, as more of the undead died against our groups' weapons.

My sister's harsh laughter once again bought my focus back to her craziness, what is up with this girl? Doesn't she get that her army of undead was dying all over again. Still laughing and muttering under her breath, she pointed down the steps where I watched one of the goblins go down, then a shifter, but how were we being destroyed by them? As more undead popped up from the ground, I thought, where are these bodies all coming from?

That's when I noticed that as her warriors were cut down; they came back up again whole and in one piece and were jumping right back into the fight. As I watched this, I saw another goblin go down under a vicious cut from an undead sword, only for that goblin to stand up and now attack his former comrades in arms. "You sssee now, little girl, that your friendsss can't win, for as they die they join mine to kill your other friendsss."

"Yeah well, if swords won't kill these guys, let's see what a little fire will do to your army," I said as I threw down a wall of flame along the front of my sister's army. Backing up the last few feet from the top of the steps, all that was left of our group watched as undead bodies burned in the flames.

Chuckling and still muttering under her breath, my sister just pointed once again and, to the horror of everyone in our group, we could see her soldiers moving through the wall of bright flames I had put up to protect my friends and me. As the bodies moved closer up the steps, I desperately tried to think of something to save my friends.

Listening to Rli muttering under her breath, controlling the undead before us, I wished that I had her power to control earth as she did, to control the undead and save my friends . . . "Oh yeah, you little witch, that's the way it's going to be is it; well, see how you like this," I said as I lurched at Rli, grabbing both her bony arms in my hands and hoping like heck this worked.

"NOOOOOOOOOO!" she screamed. "No! My power; my magic!"

I held on tight to her, feeling her struggle against my grip; feeling something like a flow of electricity running up my arms and flowing into my inner core. As I leached my sister's magic from her, the hood of her robe fell from head, revealing a face full of fright and fear.

"No, please, no," she whispered as she slowly sank down to the floor.

Never releasing my grip, I watched as she faded. "I'm sorry, Rli, I truly never wanted it like this," I whispered back to her. I could feel a tear slowly trickle down my cheek as the last of Rli disappeared, leaving me holding an empty robe that smelled as of an old, enclosed, musty, moldy room recently opened to the fresh air. "I really am sorry, please forgive me, sister."

"Princess," a voice whispered over my shoulder, "are you all right?"

I dropped the robe that Rli had worn; stood and turned to look at my friends as they gathered around me. "Yeah, I'm fine, just didn't want it to end that way is all. Are they gone? I mean, have the undead left now that Rli is gone?"

Da stepped up and put his hands on my shoulders, "Yes, Princess, they stopped as soon as you grabbed her, and when she went, they did too. I'm sorry for your loss, even though it had to be done. You do understand that, right?"

Sighing, I looked around at what was left of our group, thought of the losses that we had getting here and for the ones lost after we arrived. "Yeah Da, I know, just still don't like the feeling like I could have done more than stealing the magic and essence from my own sister." Sitting down on the throne, I looked around the room trying to figure what was next now that I was out of trouble with the one who had started this whole mess. "I think I just need to sit and think for second. Okay, guys?"

Ro stepped up alongside Da and looked me up and down as though double checking that I was telling the truth about being all right and that I was still really in one piece. "The rest of us will check the castle, but I want Mr. Blue and the troll to stay with you, just in case we missed any northern goblins on the way in."

"Yeah, that's fine Ro, I'll just wait here for you," I said. I didn't really care who he left as long as they would give me a little time, even semi by myself to gather my thoughts together.

Soon the room was empty except for me and my companions. Scom was sitting quietly a few steps below me, as if in his own world and Mr. Blue was sniffing and snuffling among a couple of piles of old bones that were set on each side of the throne. He was worrying some old tough meat off of the bones like a puppy playing with scraps thrown to him. Reaching down I gave the old fuzz ball a pat on the head. "How did we ever get into this mess, old guy?" He just glanced up with a contented look, wagged his tail, and went back to worrying the bone between his teeth.

"It is not your fault, Princess. You cannot be responsible for other's misdeeds. You understand right, Princess?" Scom looked up at me from where he sat, looking as sad as I felt.

"Thanks, Scom, I do know what you mean. I just need to find who caused this trouble with my sister. She said her teacher was the one that told her to bring me back. I think, Scom, I need to talk to . . ."

"Me, Princess," whispered a voice from the dark shadows behind the throne.

Jumping up with a start, I tried to look into the deep darkness from where the mysterious voice issued from. "Who's there?" I asked as Mr. Blue moved between me and the shadows, giving a low growl of warning.

As a dark figure detached itself from the deeper darkness at the back of the throne, its feet seemed to float inches above the floor as it glided toward me. "I am Rli's teacher and I have come back to take the both of you to my mistress," the figure said as she stopped before me and Mr. Blue.

Looking Rli's teacher up and down in her dark robes, hiding the face and body beneath in shadows, I gave a small laugh. "What is it with you guys? Are black robes the new chic look in this world? I mean, come on, does anyone wear any color around here?"

"Silence you, where is your sister?" she demanded, her voice now rising above the whisper it had been at a few seconds ago.

Humm, maybe I was starting to get to the old girl. "She had to step out for awhile, but she gave me her magic powers as they are, to hold." About then, I could feel Scom move up to my side and grab hold of my hand. His touch drove away what little fear that was still in me and let me focus on the creature in front of me that had started all this trouble between my sister and me.

Stepping to the side and putting my other hand on Mr. Blue's arm, I felt that if anyone needed to be scared of something it was the one standing before me, because right now I could feel the anger growing inside me at this thing that was acting as though it controlled my fate. "All right listen you; I know you're the cause of the problems between my sister and me. I know you had her bring me back, and because of that I had to get rid of her..."

CHAPTER 18

Suddenly it was dark, as dark as if light didn't exist. I could feel nothing where just seconds ago each of my hands gripped one of my friend's hands. I couldn't even feel those hands nor any part of my body. It was as if I was not alive, just a soul floating in a vast nothingness.

Then light, a flickering light, given off from a fire as seen in the far distance. I took a few steps toward it, then stopped and looked down, seeing that I once more had a body. Looking around I could see I was in a long room with a low ceiling. At the one end, where the fire was, sat a chair, a large white chair shining in the flickering light. Looking around as I walked toward the flames, I caught, out the corner of my eyes, figures moving, gliding along the walls. These people were hard to see straight on, as if they weren't really there, but just spectral images of a real person. But looking from the side, I could catch glimpses of them as they moved about.

Where the heck am I and how do I get back to the castle? I thought, and boy is Ro going to be sooo mad at me. Now how do I explain this one? I had finally reached the fire and was coming around the chair where I could see a lovely older lady sitting up straight in her chair, with a look of anticipation on her face.

The lady had long golden hair cascading around her shoulders, falling over the red short shift that she wore. Her eyes, though, were as black as a starless night or of a dark, deep well that the light cannot penetrate. She had sort of a dreamy looking smile on her face that did not seem to reach those dark, deep eyes.

"So you have come to me at last Rli?" she asked.

"I'm not Rli; I'm Ceri, her sister. Who might you be?" I answered, figuring there was no use beating around the bush here. I had a funny feeling that whatever was going on here, I might not like too well, so might as well get some answers while I could.

The dreamy smile left her face and a look of disappointment descended. "What do you mean you are not Rli? Where is her teacher?" she asked as she stood from her chair, looking around the room. None of the spirits or ghosts, or whatever they were reacted to the lady's words.

In fact, none even flinched when a dark shadow appeared in front of the fire. "I am here, my mistress," the voice from the throne room answered in a harsh whisper from the shadow. "Rli is no more, my mistress, and this creature, her sister Ceri is the one that took her magic and powers – thereby destroying her."

The shadow's mistress turned her black eyes toward me. "Well, when she puts it that way, it does sound pretty bad, but you had to be there and know the whole story," I stammered as I backed up from that cold gaze. "I mean, she didn't say that my sister wasn't quite all there and that her so-called teacher put her up to bringing me back and killing me, does she?"

Looking over, I could see the shadow flinch a little at

my words. Hopefully that meant I had scored some points for my side, because I had this funny feeling that I was once again in a fight and wasn't sure what the rules were or what the fight was about.

"My mistress . . .," the dark voice whispered then stopped with a wave of her mistress' hand. Not a movement or any sound now issued from the robed darkness. It was as if no life or spark was within the shadow anymore, just coldness as in death or a blankness, of nothing in that spot.

Slowly the lady turned back to me, her gaze now taking in my whole being. Looking me up and down, it felt like she could see inside me – how I felt, my dreams, and my thoughts. "I can look at you and see that you are not like your mother or your sister, but that still does not make you a good person," she said in a haunting voice. "Though provoked, you still stole what was not yours to have."

Standing up taller and looking the lady in those dark eyes, I tried to sound confident and said, "I did what I needed to survive and to help my friends. It was my sister's teacher, your whatever she is that started this problem. So if anyone is to be blamed, you could say it falls on you two, don't you think?"

She stood there looking at me, which seemed like forever, before she finally answered me. "You may be right; this one I can see had her own agenda now." With that the lady waved her hand and there was an eerie scream and the dark robes fell to the ground as if what was once in them was no more, while a white wisp of a person appeared before us.

"Once again you are like the rest, never to be whole again, like the others around you," the lady said pointing at the apparition who was once my sister's teacher. As the ghost, spirit, or whatever it was disappeared, her mistress sat down once again in her chair and stared into the fire.

I stood there waiting to see what would happen next, but soon got the feeling that I was being ignored, or maybe that the lady had forgotten I was even there. This was seriously starting to get annoying. "Umm listen, could you answer some questions?" I asked as I moved myself in her line of sight.

Her eyes once again focused on me. "Do not anger me, mortal," she whispered, "just leave my realm." Once again her eyes started to lose focus as she stared through me at the fire.

"I'm sorry, I'm not trying to peeve you off or anything, but I am caught up in something that I have no idea what the rules are, where I am or who everyone is; so a little help would be appreciated."

The lady sat in her chair for a long while, then with a sigh she slowly looked at me once again, but this time, as I looked, I noticed that her eyes had softened as she pointed to a small stool that had suddenly appeared before her chair. "Sit and I will tell you all I know about you and yours."

CHAPTER 19

In a high towered castle set upon soaring, frosty mountains, a glittering robed figure moves through winding paths. Some are open to the air where the wind blows across, threatening to sweep all that moves through them into the abyss below. The towers reach high into the sky, some disappearing into the clouds above, the light shining off each tower as if each was built of diamonds. Small figures can be seen winging between towers and the clouds around them.

The figure soon reaches the center tower and enters the large, airy throne room. In the center of the room stands a crystal ball that sits on a pedestal of silver. As she looks at the crystal, the figure sweeps her hood back revealing long silver hair that shapes a sharp-featured face with eyes the color of yellow with slit pupils like an eagle. "Soon my sister, you will be mine. Rli may have failed, but I will not. I will have you as soon as my pets will take you." As she gazes into the crystal, she gasps in dismay one second and then laughs at what she sees the next.

———————————————

I sat down on the stool, hoping now I would get the whole scoop on what was going on around this place. The trip back to this world was getting weirder and weirder by the minute and I felt like I was going to lose my mind if I couldn't get back home soon. I was even beginning to think it might not be a bad idea to look around for some ruby slippers if nothing else worked.

As these thoughts flickered through my mind, the lady sitting above me gave another deep sigh and started in on my family tale. "You know you are half witch and half demon, right?"

"So I've heard," I said thinking tell me something I don't already know.

Looking a little perturbed, she continued, "Your mother was a full witch who was banished to this world as punishment. In fact, she was banished from the world you were hidden in."

"Wait a minute; I know there are people who think they are witches, but they don't really have real magic power, do they?" I asked thinking back to home and how some of the people at school dressed and acted like being a witch was a real thing. "Are you telling me that those kids all dressed in black were for real?"

She looked down at me with a small smile. "No, most witches are people who believe in magic, and try to live in tune with the world around them. Then there are others who go to the extreme in their beliefs, and then there are the ones born with magic inside of them, the true witch."

"Oh okay, I see, I guess. Makes sense, so my mother was one of these true, magical witches; is that what you're saying?"

"Yes, that's what I'm telling you."

"Okay, she got banished here, and then what happened?"

For a second I didn't think she would answer me, but she looked around her room and then back at me and continued with her story. "Once your mother figured out her magic was even more powerful here, she took over and made her own kingdom. She took a different husband and had four daughters from each one."

"What happened to our fathers? Didn't they complain about this?" I asked.

As I spoke, I could see a tear slowly trickle down her cheek. "No, as each child grew up; their father disappeared – never to be seen again."

"Not very bright of these guys, was it? You would think after the first or even second one went missing, these guys would have gotten a clue," I said with a smirk on my face that soon disappeared as I looked at the lady's eyes, which once again were going dark and empty.

"Your sister's father was my consort. Your mother, with her magic, stole each man's heart, used them and then disposed of them."

Oops, stepped in that one, I thought. It was time to pull the old feet out of the mouth before I really peeve this gal off. "Sorry miss, I didn't mean to be so flippant; sometimes it's just my way of dealing with things I don't understand," I whispered, hoping that that would pacify her.

She stared at me deeply for a few more seconds and then I could see the darkness slowly leave her eyes once more. "It is all right; it is just that you favor your mother more than any of your sisters, which makes it hard to talk to you sometimes." She shook her hair slightly and then looked at me again with some sympathy. "Anyway, where was I? Oh yes, your mother had your sisters, and she her powers grew stronger. When your sisters were sent to their own places, your mother demanded that we send teachers to help guide and tutor your sisters in their particular powers." A small smile appeared on the storyteller's face, "Then she had you, and that's when the trouble started for your mother."

She reached down and cupped my face in her hand. "Such a small thing you were to cause so much trouble."

I could feel the heat climb my face from embarrassment. "I didn't mean to cause trouble then."

The lady sat back with a small laugh like the tinkle of tiny bells. "No, I imagine you didn't, but trouble you did cause for your mother and then for your sisters. Your sisters became worried about your ability, for they were afraid to lose their powers to you. Your mother, they banished because she had you in the first place, and her power was weakened." The lady shook her head again and looked down at her feet. "So much wasted power that could have been used for good," she sighed and whispered wistfully.

"And me, I asked, how—"

"You were sent away for protection. It was thought that maybe you weren't as bad as the rest of your family, maybe you could use your powers for something other than being evil," she said, once again looking down at my face.

"Then why did my sister's teacher, your minion or whatever she was, have my sister bring me back?"

"Unfortunately, your family is not the only evil that lives in our world, and to my shame I was too distracted by my loss to pay attention to all that was going on around me. I ignored those that thought they could rule better then I in this realm." The lady had a look as she talked as if she was wakening from a long sleep or dream. As she talked more and told me about my family, I could her voice getting stronger with each word.

"Well that's nice that you got rid of your problem, but what about me? Does this mean I get to go home now?" I asked in a hopeful voice, thinking that maybe this was someone that could get me out of this place, and back where I belonged.

"But you are home, here in this world. This is where you were born, where your place is, this is home for you," she said, taking my hand in hers, standing and taking me with her as she stepped off the platform that held her chair. "You need to see your other sisters, to take their powers and change this world into something good. The ones who live here deserve to live in a world without your sisters as rulers, they—."

"Yeah, but how do you know that I might not be like them deep down, I mean they are my family, right?" I voiced the concern that had been dogging me since I found out about my family.

The lady stopped in midstride and looked deep into my eyes as a glittering shimmer lit up around her. "Each person makes their own lives, their own choices; there is no omnipresent being taking us by the hand and leading us to our choices. If you live for good, you do good deeds; just as to live for evil, you do evil. No one forces these choices upon you, but you."

"Well okay then, ummm, how about at least sending me back to my sister's castle then. I mean I like what you've done with the place, but everyone will be wondering where I went to, you know? That is, if we're okay and everything, you know."

She just looked at me and smiled like the cat that ate the mouse. "Don't worry, your friends won't miss you; but you are right, you need to go back for only the truly dead can stay in my realm."

Looking around at the flickering shadows of people as they walked around us, I asked, "So is this heaven or hell, I mean you're not—"

At this she threw her head back and laughed, cutting off my question. Then still chuckling she waved her arms around encompassing all around us, "You are thinking as in your old world, in this world this is where the dead go to await rebirth. I gather the souls in my realm, how they get back into the world of the living depends on how they lived their previous lives, but now you must go back to your friends."

CHAPTER 20

"But wait—," I shouted but, with a sudden kick in my midsection, I was once again in nothingness, blankness, and then I was standing in the throne room of Rli's castle touching the side of Mr. Blue and holding Scom's hand, listening to a small voice talking to me.

"What did you do, Princess, to make the big, scary voice go away like that? One second it's there and the next it's gone. You know what I mean, Princess?" Scom was chattering away in his usual shotgun way of talking, with no breath in between words.

"Ummm, how long was I gone, Scom?" I asked, puzzled by his lack of concern at my absence and subsequent return.

"What do you mean, Princess? You haven't moved from this spot since we heard that voice out of the shadows," Scom said, now looking as puzzled as I felt. "Are you okay, Princess? Do you need to sit down or something?"

Now hearing a touch of concern creep into the little guy's voice, I couldn't decide if I was losing my mind or just having another dream within a dream because I still wasn't sure if this world was real or not. "Scom, in this world is there a realm of the dead with a very beautiful woman in charge?"

Scom gave me an exasperated look. "Why, of course, Princess everyone knows that, but it is a place where you go when you die to await your next life. It is ruled by the mistress of the realm, a place you want to wait a long, long time to visit. You know what I mean, right Princess?"

"Yeah, Scom, I do know what you mean, and you're right, I hope it's a while before I see that place." Smiling, I turned around and looked at the entrances to the throne room, for we could hear the others returning from their search of the castle grounds.

Straightening up from the crystal, she raises her silver mane to the cold air and gives a high piercing call, then once more gazes deep down into the mist swirling inside the crystal, listening to the answering call from the air around her. "It is now my turn, Ceri," she whispers with a small chuckle.

She looks up at the sound of hooves hitting the tower floors and the sliding of wings against her creatures' bodies. "My pets, you need to bring me a guest to visit," she bellows as she walks toward the ones waiting to fulfill her desires.

Each of her pets acknowledges their mistress with a snort; one of wind, and one of frost. Walking between each creature, she runs her hands down their bodies; both the same, but different. Both creatures look like horses; one white, the other blue; white for snow and frost, blue for the air and wind. As she passes their shoulders, each shifts their massive wings across their backs to allow their mistress room to move down their bodies. She turns as she reaches their flanks and now moves back toward their heads once again, running her hands against their sleek bodies.

Touching their faces she reaches up and tenderly pulls an ear of each of her pets closer to her face where she whispers to them. "My sister may soon want to travel. Once she leaves Rli's castle, take some soldiers and I want her brought here to me, no matter the cost. If she doesn't leave the castle, then take her from there."

Each of her pets snorts once again in understanding and shakes their manes, while rustling their wings; anxious to take flight and carry out their mistress' bidding. "Go!" she yells. "Don't return until you have her." With that each creature takes flight into the night sky, soon to become lost in the clouds.

Sitting up from my warm furry bed of demon protector, I thought that maybe there were some advantages to having my big buddy as big as he is rather than as a little stuffed bear. Even though I missed having him to curl up with in my arms, he does make a pretty good pillow and bed when all you have to sleep on is rock.

I know that Rli was the Princess of earth, but you would think my sister would at least have something soft to sleep on. No wonder she was always so grumpy when she was around. Now if only I could find the little princess' room around here, the day could get started on the right foot.

Stretching my arms over my head as I searched around the room, I noticed something new on my arm that I hadn't noticed yesterday in all the commotion. "Oh shoot, not another one, how the heck am I getting tattoos without noticing them?" Sure enough on my arm, under my old tattoo there was a round brown globe with a snake encircling it. In the snake's mouth, like my dragon tattoo, was a jewel except that this one looked like a black diamond.

Hearing something scurrying behind me, I turned to find a smaller version of the bugs that attacked us in the tunnels coming up through a hole in the ground that was hidden just behind the base of the throne. Flicking my newly tattooed arm at the bug, I watched as it froze in place and then turned to stone. "Wow! That was an interesting result."

Walking over to the hole, I looked around to see if anyone had noticed that little trick or that I had taken to talking to myself, but both Mr. Blue and Scom were still deeply asleep. Well good, I thought, a girl should have some secrets.

Looking down where the bug had come up from, I could see that there was a small entrance with steps leading down into the dark. Looking around once more and seeing only my sleeping friends; with a quick thought I lit a small flame in my hand and started down the steps to see where they led. It's pretty cool that, with a thought, I could change my powers between fire and earth.

The steps stopped not far past the entrance to the hole before a closed, stone door. On the door was a handprint embedded into the stone face, and above the door was a symbol just like the new decoration on my arm. I had gone this far so what the heck, I thought, as I laid my hand with the snake tattoo on it into the depression hoping this would open the door and not start the morning off with any new troubles.

Nothing happened for a second; I felt the door tremble under my hand and then it totally disappeared on me. Walking forward, I found myself in a small, dark room that had unlit torches on the walls and piles of books on a table in the center of the room. There was a small whisper of a wind. Or was it a voice from far away, floating through the air? As I walked further into the room, the wind (or voice) soon disappeared into the dark.

I could feel a wave of power emanating from the table; power that was seeking, looking to undermine and destroy the light around it. Backing out of the door to the edge of the bottom step, I thought that there was no way anyone else besides my sister was going to get her hands on these books anymore. With a flick of my arm, I started to throw balls of flames into the room. As the books started to burn, I heard eerie, ghostly cries issue from the volumes. As each of the books burned, the cries died, but each emitted a grey specter that floated up from the ash and then disappeared with a puff of smoke. As the last specter disappeared, the door to the room appeared again closing off access to the mess I had just created.

Walking back up the short set of steps, I had a sudden thought: I hoped that those books didn't belong to the mistress of the under realm, because she probably wouldn't be too happy with me burning her library; no matter how bad those books were. Well, no use crying over it now, the damage was done. Coming off the top step, I pointed my new tattooed arm at the hole hiding that ugly room and sure enough, with a flick of my arm, the hole disappeared as it was filled with solid stone. "There! That should take care of that little problem." Having one power seemed to be pretty cool, having two powers was becoming quite helpful in this new world.

"Princess, where are you?" sounded like Ro was looking for me; well, time to get back to my friends and find a way home, I guess.

"I'm over here, Ro," I answered as I walked around from the back of the throne's base. "Just looking for the

little girl's room, Ro." Looking around, I could see that my
two sleeping buddies were just waking up, so I was pretty
sure that no one had noticed my little adventure.

"Well, can you come up to the top room? We would
like to figure out what we are going to do next, Princess,"
Ro said as he looked around the room and sniffed the air.
Have you been burning something Princess, because it
smells—"

"Yeah, just give me a couple of seconds, Ro, and I'll be
right there okay, really just need to take care of some
morning functions here."

"Oh right yeah, I'll be waiting upstairs for you then."
Ro gave me a long look then marched back up the stairs he
had just come down.

Looking around the room, Scom gave me a puzzled
look and said, "I smell it too, Princess. You know what I
mean don't you, Princess? It does smell like something was
burn—"

Giving Scom a push toward the stairs to get him
moving after Ro, I cut him off saying, "Come on Scom,
and give a girl some privacy here. Now up the steps you go,
I'll be right up there in a second."

"Oh okay, Princess, yes I understand," the little fellow
said as he marched up the stairs in Ro's wake.

Turning around I eyed the big furry bundle sitting there
looking at me with big, round, curious eyes. "And one
word out of you, big guy, and you're out of here next," I
said as I went to find a private spot, a chamber pot, a hole
in the ground, anything to relieve my greatest mounting
pressure right now. Then I headed up to take care of my
second greatest need – food.

Afterward, much relieved and well fed, I finally found
out what Ro wanted with me earlier. Seems like the shifters
were ready to go home and wanted me to return to their

valley with them; the goblins wanted me to stay and protect them from any big, bad uglies that might still be hanging around the area. Either way, all this girl wanted was to find a way home.

"Well Princess, stay here with goblins or come home with us – those are your options," Da rumbled in his thick, loud voice. "At least living with us you would be safer than staying here and playing guardian to a bunch of goblins."

Err, the new leader of the southern goblins, jumped up, seemingly taking exception to this slight on goblin manhood and tried to go nose to nose with Da, but only coming up to the big shifter's chest even though Da was sitting down, he instead turned to talk to me. "Princess, you would be revered and honored if you stay here with us and not go with these animals," he sneered taking in the shifters with a sweep of his hand.

Da jumped up and stepped toward Err. "Animals, huh, you little green piece of—"

"ENOUGH!" I yelled, cutting off the big shifter's tirade in mid burst. Everyone in the room looked at me as if I were a prize in the Cracker Jack box, "I have decided what I am going to do. I am going to my own castle and try to find a way home."

There was silence then. Scom, who was sitting next to me, reached up and tugged on my shift. "That might not be a good idea, Princess, since your castle sits in the middle of the dragon lands. If you know what I mean, Princess?"

Yeah I knew exactly what he meant, but since that was where they had sent me to my world in the first place, I figured that was where I needed to be to get back home.

"You are home here in this world, Princess," Ro said in a quiet voice, sharing a look with the others in the room.

"No, I was born here, but my real home is in that other world, the normal world where there is no magic, goblins,

or shifters and such. Look at me, I don't belong here."
Everyone looked at me with a puzzled look as my wings
rustled behind my back. "Well okay, maybe now, the way I
look I fit in, but this isn't the real me."

"But Princess," Scom said looking up at me with big,
wide, puppy dog eyes, "this is the real you."

"Fine, this is the real me, but I still just want to go home
where everything isn't trying to eat or kill me." With that I
turned my back on the crowded room and walked out to
find a spot where I could be homesick and miserable by
myself.

My big furry buddy, Mr. Blue, followed me around as I
wandered the castle and made a nice back rest as I settled
in a small niche on the corner of the castle walls. From
there I could look out at the landscape, but my mind was
focused solely on thoughts of getting back to the normal,
boring life I knew.

I sulked in my private spot all day and even turned Mr.
Blue back into teddy bear form to cuddle. It was dark by
the time I heard small footsteps moving toward my hidden
spot.

A small voice squeaked out of the night, "There you are,
Princess; all of us were getting worried about you."

"I'm fine, Scom, I just wanted some alone time," I said
as I stared over the wall.

"I understand, Princess, but it is food time and you have
not eaten all day. Please come down and have some food,
won't you?" Giving me a look of concern, the little guy
moved closer to me and laid a small hand on my shoulder.
"We all worry about you, Princess, and starving yourself
with worry won't help you. You know what I mean, right
Princess?

"Yeah, Scom, I do know what you mean," as my empty
stomach gave a quiet rumble, "I'll be right down for some

food, okay? Just give me a few more seconds by myself."

"All right Princess, but please come down soon."

"I will Scom, promise," I told his departing back.

A few minutes later my stomach gave a not so lady-like rumble and I decided that maybe some food was in order to, if not improve my mood, then, at least, to quiet my stomach. Standing up, looking at the night sky, I could see several something's flying high above the castle.

As I stood there watching the figures circling, coming closer and closer to where I was, I could see that they looked like . . . men with wings? Now that was weird, even for a place like this. As they got larger, I could see that each figure was armed with a short bow and funny looking spear and what looked like silver armor that shined brightly in the moonlight.

Thinking that I should let someone know about these weird creatures flying above the castle, I started to turn when I felt a cold breath of air seep over my body. As blackness overcame my mind, I could hear yells and screams around me and my last thought was well here we go again.

CHAPTER 21

Coming out of the castle's armory, Ro looked around the area at the bodies of fallen goblins and shape shifters that littered the castle yard. Among the fallen friends and allies, he could see a few of the strange, winged warriors that had attacked their stronghold. Pale winged men that wore silver armor with weapons that consisted of a short bow and, instead of the sword that most warriors he knew carried, each was also armed with a spear that had a lethal point at one end and a wicked hook at the other. Ro stood in silence, taking in the bodies as the sound of wings faded in the black night.

"Ro, Ro, they have the Princess!" a small frightened voice sounded from the night.

With a sigh, Ro turned to the small body staggering up to him from the other side of the grounds. "I know Scom. I saw her as they flew away with her."

"Then we must do something Ro, we must find her. You know what I mean, right Ro? I mean, the Princess, she can't be dead can she, Ro?"

"No, I don't think she is dead, Scom, I think they want her alive – at least for now. Come on Scom, first we need to tend to the wounded then…"

"But what of the Princess, Ro?" The small troll looked at the shifter with haunted eyes.

"Right now we need to help our wounded before we can help her," Ro said as he guided the small warrior toward those who needed their attention.

I slowly woke up in the cold darkness, feeling the iciness of the chains that encircled my arms and legs. Moving with deliberate caution, I could feel the cold metal chaffing against my skin and sending shivers up my already freezing body. Wherever I was this time upon waking, I would guess it wasn't a warm and fuzzy place to live in.

I didn't know who bought me here or if anyone was in the room with me. Cupping my hands together, I could muster only a small ball of flame to warm me and to give me enough light to look around. It seemed that once again my magic was limited by some other power. Looking around to my left and slowly sliding around, I could see I was in a small windowless room of rock. There was a door in front of me and to my right . . . "Oh Crap!" Sitting next to me, on my right, was a frozen roommate. Sliding as far from him as my chains would allow, I could see that he looked like the same type of creature that had been flying over the castle earlier.

Seeing that my new roommate and I were the only ones imprisoned in the room, I tried to put a little more power into the flames cupped in my hands. It managed to grow enough to light up the room. I could feel the warmth throughout my body grow and warm the surrounding air of the room I was now in.

Looking closer at my icy companion, I could see that the cold had been his undoing and vowed not to let the warmth in my hands die down. He sat huddled tight into a small ball chained to the walls as I was, his wings wrapped around his body as if to hold in the heat as long as he could at the end. Sliding closer to the poor creature to get a better look, I noticed that what I took for a fur coat was actually his skin and that he looked like a giant winged man covered from head to toe in fur.

Bringing the light once more up to his face to get a closer look at his features, I once again slid as far back as my chains would allow for two piercing blue-grey eyes were now staring at me with curiosity.

"Who are you to wake me from my hibernation?" his voice rumbled as he slowly stretched out his body and his wings as far as his chains would allow, all the while taking in his surroundings. "I see I am still in my cage, so my daughter has not relented then."

"Who are you exactly?" I asked my now unfrozen companion.

"I am Car, the king of the Cars actually, before my daughter put me in this stone cage," he said as he straightened his body and his wings spread out as far as the cramped room would allow.

"So your name is Car, and your people are named Car?" I asked in puzzlement.

He glanced at me with a look of amusement on his face. "The people are named after their king; my name is Car, so my people are named Car, of course."

Peering down at me closely with his piercing eyes, he suddenly chuckled, "I know you, you are the young one that disappeared; the one everyone was trying to find, the one that would bring down my daughter and her sisters when you came back to this world."

"Oh you mean you and my mother, uh well you know, uh…"

"Yes I do know, very well," he said with a smile and a

slight shrug of his shoulders as in apology. He stared off into the past with a wistful look. "She may have been bad in her world, probably very bad, but she was beautiful and hard to resist and very, very good in this world."

"Uh yuck, too much info there, big guy; that's my mother your referencing there."

"Then you should not ask questions you do not want the answers to, young one."

"Yeah ok that's my bad, but you caught me by surprise there. I thought you were, you know, frozen and all dead and stuff. So what's with the coming back to the living?"

"My people have lived in this land for a long time. We have adapted to the cold so that we can hibernate inside ourselves until the warmth wakes us up. It is a defense from the brutal weather that has allowed us to survive the cold of this land."

"Oh, okay, can see where that would be helpful on those cold winter nights. How did you get wherever here is if you're the big boss of these people?"

He looked around the small room and then looked down on me once again, "When your mother sent each of her offspring to rule over a section of the world, we fought and each leader of that kingdom lost. I escaped my fate, some were not so lucky. When I heard that your mother was banished and that you had disappeared, I came back to fight once again for my rightful place; forgetting that there are always some who would sell out for any price. When I lost against your sister, my daughter sent me down here where I was to be kept out of sight and out of mind."

"Your own daughter sent you down here to die; now that's one nasty temper."

"To die, to hibernate, as long as I was out of the way, she did not care which. Now tell me how you got to be in this place, little one?"

"It's a long story."

"Well little one, I don't see that we are going anywhere soon, do you?"

"Yeah, you do have a point." So I leaned back against the now warmed walls and settled in and gave an account of my life in my old world and then finished with my little adventures up to the point where I had awakened the big guy from his long winter's nap. With nary a word or gesture, he sat through my story giving me his undivided attention until I hit the end of my tale. "Well what do you think big guy? I'm in big trouble again, right?"

Shaking his head and giving me a grim look, the big guy gave me the answer I had been dreading. "Yes little one you are in trouble. For your sister does not want you around as she did not want her mother or, for that fact, me in her life."

I leaned back against the wall and sighed. "Just great, my family life really sucks here. No matter what world I live in, there's always something, but at least back home, though I may have been a foster kid, I didn't have monsters looking to eat me."

Car stared at me with a look of amusement on his face. "Just because you didn't see the monsters in your world doesn't mean they weren't there, little one, or that they were not out to get you either."

A look of puzzlement must have been written all over my face because he reached out and gave me what I took as a reassuring pat on the head. Just before I could ask him what he was talking about, the lock on the door to our accommodations rattled and in walked three armed warriors – one of them bearing a globe giving off a weird, white light.

The biggest of the three looked at Car with contempt and loathing. "You will not move Car or we will hurt the little one."

"I will not move Sor, there is no reason to hurt her. She should not be here; she is not a part of this world."

"The Princess will decide what she is and what she isn't Car, not you. You gave that right up when you fled the first time."

"Friends of yours?" I asked the big guy.

"No. Remember I said there are always some that have a price? Well this is the one that my daughter found who would betray me for a price."

"Oh."

"You will put out the flame in your hand, little one, and come with us." I started to try to make the flame bigger in my hand, figuring that if they thought they were going to take me anywhere they were going to have a fight on their hands. I may be smaller than these guys, but I figured between Car and I we could take them down or least singe some wings before they could take us out.

Looking at Car to see if he was ready for a fight, he just shook his head and smiled a sad smile. "No, little one, now is not the time to fight; that time will come soon."

"Always the coward, Car, always ready to run." Sor said with a sneer. "Take her; the Princess awaits."

I snuffed out the flames, figuring what the heck, I wanted to see my sister anyways, and thinking maybe I could get her to see that all I wanted to do was just go home and get out of everyone's hair. After all, I wasn't the one whose idea it was to come to this weird, tripping place. The other two warriors grabbed hold of me once the chains were off and carried me out of the room I had been held in. "Hey what about Car, the king, you can't just leave him here."

"Quiet little one, you do not command us!" As Sor shut the door to the room, I could see Car, in the darkness once again, curling himself into his wings to hibernate in the cold that would soon engulf the prison he was in.

As the door clicked shut, I kicked the guard on my left in the leg and, as he let go, I swung around and got a good fist into the midsection of the guy holding me on the right; but before I could turn around and blast their leader, I felt like I had been hit with a sledge hammer and I flew into the brick wall behind me. "ENOUGH, with this foolishness! Let's get her to the Princess!" Sor yelled as he picked me up and threw me back at the guards like a sack of laundry. The two guards had now recovered from my slight attack and looked at me with daggers in their eyes for daring to make them look like buffoons.

I looked at Sor with as much venom as I could muster. "You know, it's not nice to hit a girl and, when this is over, I will pay you back."

All three warriors looked at me and started to laugh at my bravado. "I can't wait for that day, little one. Who knows, maybe the Princess will give you to me and my men when she is done with you. Then we will see just how brave you are in a fight."

"Yeah, laugh it up big boys. Just remember – the bigger they are the harder they fall; and when I'm done with you three, you will all fall hard." With that oath spilling from my lips, and hoping I could keep that promise, they jerked me off my feet and marched me to see my sister.

Wherever they were keeping me it must have been down deep. We walked up many ramps, passing people like Car and Sor who all seemed to be in a hurry going about on different chores and assignments. That none of the people gave me or my guards a second glance told me that there had been others before me who had taken this trip. In fact, it seemed like all the others did not want to make any eye contact with me or the guards taking me to my meeting. In fact most of the people I saw looked downright scared of my guards. That, I thought, did not bode well for the outcome of meeting my sister or for getting her to send me home.

Ro looked around at the mixed group of shifters, goblins and other creatures that were marching by. All were prepared to fight to save the Princess, knowing that they were probably too late to save her, but that they would at least avenge her. He watched as a line of northern goblins marched by, surprised as any when they had showed up at the castle ready to pledge allegiance to the new Princess, only to find that she had been taken. Then a ragged line of trolls followed along behind the goblins, lead by Scom. Though they were not as skilled at battle as the shifters and goblins, he could see the look of determination in their leader's eyes. Watching as the rest of the group moved by him, Ro turned as he sensed Da come up behind him.

"A fierce looking group, isn't it Ro?" the big shifter asked.

"Yeah Da, but will it matter by the time we get there?"

"We can only do what we can, nothing more. The rest is in the hands of fate, and she is a fickle vixen sometimes," Da chuckled then shrugged his shoulders. "Well at least we know where we are going from the wounded birdmen at the castle, that is something, isn't it? And look at it this way Ro, when we get there we know we'll have some more allies – if this winged person is telling the truth."

Ro sighed. "Yeah, just hope it matters to the Princess; all this to save her life. Never seen these different groups work together for a common cause is all."

Laughing, Da clapped Ro on the shoulder and pulled him down to the trail headed toward the mountains in the distance. "Well then, after we save her, we will just have to show her how needed she is here, don't we brother?"

After a long climb up to the tallest tower, my guards and I stood before two large, white, double doors. For a split second nothing happened and then slowly each door opened to reveal a cavernous, airy room. As we walked in, I could see that the center of the room held a stand with what looked like a round silver ball sitting on it.

"Hello sister," a small voice sounded like a tiny bell in the open air.

Looking up at the voice, I could see a small figure sitting high up on a throne. What is it with these girls looking down on their people from their high perches, I thought as I looked up at my sister?

"Hello there back at you, sis." I figured it wouldn't hurt to be nice until I saw what my sis had in mind for me, not that I figured whatever it was would be good for me.

"Bring her closer where I can see her better," my sister purred in a low voice.

"Yes, my Princess," all three of my guards answered as the two holding my arms grasped me tighter and lifted me from my feet and moved me closer to the throne.

As we reached the point where my sister could see me clearly, the smile plastered on her face disappeared as she looked upon me; as she saw the marks from the slap I had received. "Who marked you, my sister?" she whispered as each of my guards tensed up at the tone of her voice, suddenly ready for flight.

"My Princess, let me explain . . ." Sor started to stammer in panic as the other two of my guards started to release their grips on my arms as though they would flee at the slightest provocation.

As my sister stood, she looked down at the four of us and her voice lowered to a whisper that very nearly did not carry to us at the bottom of the steps. "Be very quiet, Sor, for right now your life and those of your men are very near its end." All three men froze as though they were rabbits looking into the eyes of a snake, ready to strike.

Slowly a pair of small wings, fine and graceful as angel's wings, unfolded from behind my sister and she floated down the steps to stand in front of our group. As she stood there, her head bowed as in prayer, I could tell that she was trying to regain her composure. Slowly she raised her head and looked at me with eyes that slowly drained of anger but had a bright, terrifying, crazy spot in each pupil.

With a sigh she whispered, "Leave us now."

If I hadn't been so worried about my own life, I would have laughed at how fast the three huge warriors moved toward the door. Each pushing the others in their haste to leave the room before my sister's temper was taken out on their hide. This, more than anything, warned me of the danger that I was in while in her presence.

"I am sorry, sister. I told them not to hurt you." My sister sighed then gave me a slight crooked smile. "If you want, I'll order them back so that you can avenge yourself on them." And with those words, her smile grew wider and her eyes lit up like a cat ready to pounce on the unsuspecting bird.

"This little old thing? Why that's not even worth my notice," I answered back touching the mark on my cheek. "Heck, I've had worse than this back home, sister dear."

The smile disappeared from her face and I saw a dark flash of annoyance in her eyes. It probably wasn't the smartest thing to do, peeving her off, but I never was smart when it came to dealing with bullies. "Now sister dear, how about we discuss why I'm here and how I get home from here, wherever here is."

"You always were direct, little sis, even when you were young. That's one of the reasons that you were sent away to that dreary non-magical world of mom's." As my sister moved around, I could see the wings flutter in the air so that she floated just above the ground, her toes just creasing the ground as she moved back and forth in front of me. "The question isn't how you get home because this is your real home you know, little sis, but why did you return from where you were sent in the first place?"

I crossed my arms across my chest and looked at my sister with as sour a look as I could muster. "Yeah well, it wasn't exactly my idea to come back to this place. I didn't even know it existed until a little while ago. So how about we stop playing games and you just send me back where I came from and then everyone is happy?"

Guess my sister wasn't too happy with my attitude because she stopped pacing in front of me and her wings started to beat faster, which caused her to rise in the air as she pointed her finger down at me. "Don't vex me, sister, for I'm not in the mood."

I don't know what a vex is, but I sure did know that I was starting to get royally peeved off by her attitude. "Listen, sissy dear, I really don't care about you and just want to get out of here and back to my normal, boring life back in my world."

My sister took a deep breath and slowly settled back to the ground in front of me. "Yes, well, I'm sorry to say little sister, that it is too late for that to happen now. You see, there is the little matter of the people who are rising up under your name."

"What are you talking about?" I stammered.

"Then there is the little matter of the dragons you have made mad by killing their king, Ernie," she continued as if I had never interrupted her. "Oh and then there is also the little matter of overthrowing Princess Rli and then taking over her kingdom now, isn't there? So you see, little sister, I would be hard pressed to send you anywhere until you answered for these crimes now, wouldn't I?"

"Crimes, my butt, you little witch. I was just protecting myself from the crazies of this world, and if you don't send me home, I'll rip those little angel wings off your back and stuff them up your . . ."

"Now, now, little sister, such language coming from a royal mouth. Have you no shame?"

"I'll show you shame, you little witch," but as I lunged toward her, to show her that what I said I would do was no threat, I bounced off of the air in front of me as if I had hit a brick wall. Once again, I found myself sitting on my butt staring up at the source of my anger. This was getting to be a tiresome habit of mine.

Looking up at her, I could see a smirk of satisfaction on her face. "Now, now, you didn't think I knew how you got rid of Rli, did you? I don't think I want to go the way our dear departed sister went, do you?"

I took a deep breath and calmed myself. Letting this little witch get to me wasn't accomplishing anything, and I would need her to get me back home. "Listen! What happened with Rli was a mistake at first and then it was just self-preservation on my part. So how about we call a truce and you send me home?" Taking another deep breath and giving her what I hoped was a humble look, I kept pressing my point since she seemed to be listening. "Once I'm home, I'll be out of everyone's hair and all your problems are solved. Remember me, sister; your little baby sister? We must have had some good times when we were younger?

Think back, was it all bad?"

My sister stood quietly for awhile, gazing down at me with a look of deep thought on her face. It was almost as if all the cruelty I had seen earlier had fled and I could see that she was a very beautiful, frightened young girl, for all the bravado she displayed in front of everyone. It was almost as if I were the oldest and she the younger of the two of us in the room. "Ceri," she whispered in a quiet, frightened little girl voice. Then she gave a deep body shudder and, with an insane cackle, the look of cruelty she wore before was back.

Dang, I thought, almost had her going my way. These sisters of mine really were not all there. It was no wonder that everyone around them was so frightened. They may be family, but these chicks were just on another plane of reality than the rest of the world, and for me that just made my life a whole lot harder.

My sister glided closer to me, staring down at me with a deep look of disgust on her face. "Oh no, you don't, little Ceri; trying to play on my heart, but I'll have you know that as the Princess of this land, my heart is as cold as the land I rule."

My shoulders fell in defeat as my sister clapped her hands together, instantly my three escorts from earlier appeared at my side, dragging me up from the ground where I sat. "Take her to her room," she said, turning away from us as she glided back toward her throne, but she had taken no more than a few steps when she whipped around like a snake striking its prey. "And remember, my sister is not to be harmed by any hand but my own." The guards quivered in their boots as they bowed at their Princess' command. "Now go," she commanded once again in dismissal.

Watching these huge idiots be frightened of a little slip

of a girl would have been funny most other times, but I wasn't so sure I could disagree with their feelings after seeing my sister up close and personal.

Thinking we were going back down to the room I had awakened in, I was a bit surprised when I was led down a different hall and soon was pushed into a room just down from the throne room. As the door closed behind me, I could hear a lock click. Well at least it was warmer here than in my first accommodations. Looking around the room, I could see another door to the side. Trying the door, I found it opened into a combination bathroom and closet with the biggest tub I ever saw inside it. Dang, you could almost hold swimming trials in that thing. Closing the door, I walked over to the window that covered the other wall. I knew that we had climbed when we were coming up here, but had no idea we were as high as we were.

Looking down, I could only get peeks of the land below because of the cloud cover that started just a few stories below my window. I quickly stepped back from the beautiful view thinking, oh heck no! Yeah, so sue me, I'm afraid of heights. Even when I used my new wings, I hadn't flown very far off the ground. Granted all my new friends thought it was funny, a creature with wings who didn't like heights, but it was my problem, not theirs. Looking around the room once again, I could feel the grime and dirt encrusting my body and thought, what the heck, since I'm here and nowhere to go, might as well see if I could swim laps in the bath, and see if any of the clothes in the room would fit me. So I headed toward the bathroom in my prison.

CHAPTER 22

As the sun set over the looming cliffs, the last rays of the day's light highlighted a lone figure sitting on a bench of rock overlooking the fires of the growing army settled in the valley below. His attention focused on a tall mountain seen in the near distance. The sound of rocks moving from the path below, leading to the solitary figure, slowly impinged on his awareness; along with the whisper of his name in the gathering dark from a familiar voice, roused him from his deep thoughts.

"Ro, you need to come down to the camp. It's not a good idea to be by yourself this close to the enemy," Da said as he hauled his considerable bulk up the last of the path he had been following. "Besides, we have new comrades in camp and maybe a way into the castle where the Princess is."

"You mean if the Princess is still alive. It has been a week since the Princess has been in her sister's fine care, Da," the figure answered as he heaved himself up from his rough seat.

Looking at his brother, a huge grin spread across his face. "She's alive all right, that's part of the news that this new group brought with them, Ro. Seems like the people in this kingdom are no happier with the leadership here than the goblins were with theirs." Da clapped a huge paw of a hand on Ro's shoulder. "They have seen the Princess and she is well, and they have a way in, if we agree to help them release their king and get rid of his daughter, the Princess Erie."

"Well, Da, I guess that just makes it easy for us, won't it."

"Yeah right," Da replied as the smile slipped from his face. "I guess nothing has gone very easy ever since the Princess Ceri has showed up, has it?"

"No, it hasn't, but what the heck, you only live once right. Now let's go see what these new guests have to say for themselves." With that both shifters headed down the path toward the camp below.

This must have been the most boring week of my life. Even swimming in the huge tub in the bathroom had gotten old after a couple of days of being locked in my high tower room. If I had my weapons I think I might even have tried to escape out my window, even with my fear of heights. Shocking what boredom will make you contemplate to escape from it. It seems that after my sister and I had our little talk, she had totally forgotten about me. The bad thing was that I was wasting my time here waiting to go home. The good thing was that I had gained the trust of the girl who bought me my meals; not enough to help me escape, of course, but enough to gain some tidbits about my sister.

I learned that my sister's name was Princess Erie, and that she had the wind at her command. I also learned from my little friend that my sister had only a small following and that for the most part the people of this land wanted to be ruled by the rightful king – Erie's father, Car, whom I had met down in the dungeons when I had first awakened a week ago. Like I said, when you're bored any little nugget of information makes the time go by. Little did I know that this boring time was about to end and looking back on it, it wasn't such a bad time after all.

I had just finished my nightly meal and was talking to my new friend, whose name was Sreni, when the door to my room was thrown open and my three guides from before came marching into the room with all the attitude of three bulls let loose in a china shop.

Sreni, the poor girl, shrunk into the corner of the room as the three warriors approached me in their most menacing manner. "You must come with us now. The Princess demands your presence." The three stopped before me as the leader of this little band reached out and grabbed my arm.

Staring at the offending hand on my arm, I slowly looked at each of the three of them. "If I were you I would remove that hand, seems like I remember that my sister wasn't too happy last time you left marks on my body." Well, you would have thought that my skin had turned to molten lead, the way his hand left my arm.

"No matter, you will come with us now," the leader said again, shifting his eyes around the room taking in the young girl hiding in the corner for the first time. "Who is she, and what is she doing in here with you?"

"She is no one and no concern of yours. I thought you were here to take me to your Princess or are you now more interested in some little slip of a girl?"

This seemed to pull their interest back to me and off the little huddled bundle in the corner. "Yes, you are right, now come with us."

I got up right away and headed toward the door when I

noticed that the attention of my three guards started to wander back toward Sreni. "Well, come on boys, no sense in keeping my sister waiting, is there?" Before I could reach the door, all three warriors were around me once again with their full attention now on getting me back to see my sister. Looking over my shoulder once again, before we left the room, I saw that the small huddled girl was now following me out the door with large frightened eyes. I gave her a small smile and wink before I lost sight of her, hoping my bravado wasn't misplaced. With the crazies I had meet so far in my family, you just never knew.

After a quick march, we were back in the same throne room I had been in before and, sure enough, there was my still-crazy big sister.

"Hello Ceri, hope you weren't too bored, cooped up in your room?" she cooed as she glided toward me. God, I thought, I have got to learn how move like that.

"Hello, Erie," this seemed to put a little hitch in her glide. "No not bored, just waiting to see what you decided to do with me. Thought maybe you came to your senses and will do the smart thing and send me home."

Erie stopped in front of me and slowly smiled a most unpleasant smile. "No Ceri, little sister, sending you home, as you call it, will be the last thing I do."

"Great, so what do you have cooking up in that crazy little brain of yours for me now, Erie?" There was a gasp behind me from my three guards. Guess no one talked to my sister that way. "Well what is it, if you aren't going to send me home, sis?"

My words brought a frown to her face, for a second, before being replaced with that cat that ate the canary smile again. "My, Ceri, you are feisty and so brave, aren't you?"

I gave a small shrug. Right now I didn't think it really mattered what I said. I figured that if I was going to go out, might as well be on my terms, right?

Erie leaned into my personal space a little more and the smile grew bigger on her face. "Remember, little sis, how I said the dragons were mad at you for killing what's his name?" She paused as in thought. "Oh yes, Ernie that was it. Well seems like they will be here in a couple of hours and they want a large piece of your hide."

"Oh!" I gulped out; seems like dragons definitely weren't a species to peeve off or likely to forget someone killing one of their own. Yeah I was in big trouble now.

Erie gave a little laugh at the look on my face as she glided toward a table I had noticed when we had walked into the room. "Ah I see you noticed that I had your weapons brought up here. Don't worry, little sis, I wouldn't let you go unarmed against three or four dragons. That just wouldn't be sporting now, would it?"

As I looked at the table, all I could think was how fast could I move before my three babysitters caught me? And could I stick one of my swords through this crazy sister of mine?

Before I could tense myself to move though a muffled boom sounded below us somewhere and I could feel the floor shake a little. All five of us froze in place and then Erie turned to her guards and yelled at them, "WELL DON'T JUST STAND THERE! GO AND FIND OUT WHAT THAT WAS!"

I just smiled as once again I saw the three guards trip over themselves as they rushed to obey the Princess' command. "Not losing it there, are we sister?"

Erie just gave me a dirty look, but then glanced at the door as we heard loud voices, yelling, and what sounded like the clash of weapons coming from the hallway outside the doors of the throne room.

As the noise increased from the unseen ruckus, my

sister grew paler and she started to move slowly toward the steps leading up to her throne. With her attention solely on the doors and the noise outside, I edged closer toward where my weapons lay. I figured that if her guards came back, I was going to go down fighting instead of putting up with any more of this garbage.

Just as I reached the table and saw my weapons laying there in all their shining glory, the doors of the throne room burst open. At the head of the crowd that now entered the throne room strode Erie's father and three people that I had thought I would never see again. For marching just behind the rightful king of this land were Ro, Da, and Scom. I gave a little laugh, for in Ro's belt I could see Mr. Blue in his raggedy old teddy bear form tucked away for safekeeping. I didn't know how much I had missed my old friend from my younger days until just that second.

As they marched into the throne room, I could see that they had quite a crowd with them that expanded and filled the area around the room. I could even see my young friend, Sreni, dancing along the edge of the crowd. She saw me and gave a shy wave which I returned with a smile and wink, though I was worried that she was too young to be caught up in all this mess.

Erie's father stopped when he was even with the table where I was standing. Looking over at me, he gave me a smile and a nod. "We meet once again, Princess." The smile faded as he turned toward his wayward daughter. "We have much to talk about, Erie," he growled as the frown deepened on his face.

Slowly, Erie glided back up the stairs as if the throne she possessed would protect her. "No father, there is no reason to talk." She took a shallow breath. "You would have been better to stay down in your cage so I would have had no need to kill you."

Out of the corner of my eyes, I saw Sreni inch her way around the edge of the crowd closer to where I stood, but my attention was once again drawn toward Erie's father as he growled at her threat. "You are all alone now, daughter. All your men are gone or they have turned their back on you and pledged to me, their rightful king."

Erie looked down at the people standing around the room and gave a contemptuous laugh. "That may be so father, but I am still more powerful with my magic than all you little creatures."

Sreni nudged through the crowd the last little bit so that she was standing at my side. The movement of the small girl bought Erie's notice once more on my being. "You, Ceri, you are the reason that this is happening."

I looked down at Sreni, then up at my older sister with little pity. "I told you, sister, that all I wanted to do was go home. You and Rli are the ones that bought these troubles down on yourselves, not me." I put my arms around Sreni to comfort her. "You could have done so much good with your power, sister, but you decided to follow another path."

Erie glared down at me then suddenly laughed. "Yeah sure, sister, like these creatures are my equal, or should I say our equal. Come Ceri, forget our past differences and let us rule these things."

Erie's father stepped forward to challenge the statements she threw down from her lofty perch. "Go ahead, father, come forward to your doom." She laughed as she raised her hands that now glowed with a light made of white-blue ice.

I stepped up in front of the crowd, now looking up at my sister and feeling my little shadow, Sreni, following me. I wished that the little thing would take a step back into the crowd, but right now I had to worry that my crazy sister wouldn't hurt the others in the room.

By now I could see that Erie had formed what look like a large snowball between her hands, but knowing this crazy chick, I'm sure getting hit by it would be worse than getting a little snow down the front of my shirt.

I looked around the room, catching the eyes of my friends and Erie's father. Seeing a slight nod from him, I once again focused on Erie. "Listen, sister, it's over; no one need get hurt . . ."

"Oh someone is going to get a little more than hurt, sister." With a flick of her hand, I saw the ball of white-blue light leave her hand and fly toward me. Time seemed to stand still forever as I watched death approach, then I noticed a small streak fly in front of me and take the light full in her small chest.

As I watched the small figure freeze and then fall to the steps to shatter in a hundred pieces, I could hear someone scream the small girl's name. Looking up at Erie as she threw her head back and laughed at the scene below her, a dark anger washed over me, burning away a part of my soul. I also felt a snap and whatever was holding my powers down shattered into a million pieces.

As Erie stood at the top of the steps laughing, I shook off the hands that tried to drag me back toward the crowd. Reaching the bottom of the steps, I could feel the heat and hatred rising up and bringing my power to a point that I had never felt before. Slinging this feeling, this need to hurt, at my sister, I flung both arms out at the figure my hatred was aimed at.

"STOP YOUR LAUGHING!" I shrieked as the power reached the figure and engulfed her; holding her in stasis as she drew her head back as if to gasp for breath.

The power left as quickly as it had come and I fell to my

knees at the bottom of the steps. Looking up through the hair that covered my face, I could see my sister roll down the steps until she was lying on the floor in front of me.

Her eyes were open as she took small shallow breaths. "You are so powerful, Ceri, we could have been so much together," she whispered.

"Why?" I whispered back as the first tears slowly slid down my cheeks.

She gave a small gasp, as if in pain. "Because they are nothing and we are everything," she slowly turned her head to look back up at the throne she had sat on.

I grasped her hand and watched as she slowly disappeared, as Rli had done. "And now you are nothing, sister." With that I sat back and, as I felt another mark glow on my arm and the tears streamed down my face, I let a wave of grief wash over me for the lost souls I had encountered in this land.

I could hear the shuffle of small footsteps behind me and the tiny, quiet whisper from a small figure, "Princess, are you all right? If you know what I mean?"

As I stood, I gathered my small friend in my arms and hugged him. "Yeah, Scom, I'm fine now that you guys have found me."

Looking around, I could see most of the people leaving the throne room while Erie's father and the rest of my friends gathered around me. Out of the corner of my eye, I could see that others were carefully moving the remains of the small girl who had saved my life. I took a deep breath and once more hugged Scom close to me. "So much waste," I whispered.

"What was that, Princess?" Erie's father said as they closed upon me.

With another sigh, I looked at all that had gathered around me. "Nothing sir, just wishful thinking on how all this could have gone down differently since I came here is all."

The big man looked deeply in my eyes as though searching for something lost. "You are not like your sisters, which in most ways is good for others, for you have compassion and do not like to hurt others." He then gave a deep sigh and continued, "But this also hurts you and others in that you do not always take action against those that deserve it, much to the detriment of yourself and sometimes others," he finished as he glanced over at the last remains of Sreni.

Not following his glance, I looked at the others. "Yeah, well, we have other problems right now than my temperament or lack thereof." This seemed to draw everyone's attention back to point. "Seems like we are going to have a visit from some dragons that are not very happy with me."

Ro stepped forward and, for the first time since he entered the room, spoke, "When are they going to get here, Princess, and how many are we going to have to fight?"

I looked around at all my friends, both old and new, as they gathered around me and made up my mind right there that no more of them were going to get hurt because of me. "They will be here soon and no one is going to fight them, especially over me."

Everyone around me raised their voice to protest my decision and I couldn't get a word in edgewise, so I just waited until the noise settled down once again. When it got quiet again, I just gave everyone what I hoped was a cool and jaunty glare. "Now who's the Princess in charge around here, as you guys keep telling me?" Everyone started to protest again, but it died down once more as I held up my hand. "Now when the dragons get here, I will meet with them and see if we can't work this little misunderstanding out."

Scom reached up and tugged my arm with a look of confusion on his face. "You know, Princess, dragons don't listen. If you know what I mean, Princess? They just like to eat their problems like Ernie tried to."

Looking down at Scom and then around at the rest of them, seeing all the concern on their faces, I knew that they were probably right, but I was determined not to lose any more of those around me. "Listen guys, we got awhile until the dragons get here and we can take it from there, ok?"

Just then the doors slammed open and in ran one of the guards looking back over his shoulder as though monsters from hell were on his tail, skidding to a stop before his king, wild-eyed and shaking the guard fell to his knees sobbing out to his king, "Dragons sir, dragons on the wall."

Everyone froze and not a sound could be heard in the throne room. I slowly looked at all the people around me and noticed the look of shock on all their faces that the guards' entrance had created. "Well I guess we go to plan B then," I said lightly, trying to break the dour mood in the room.

The king slowly looked up from the frightened guard lying at his feet and into my eyes. "And what is this plan B that you speak of, Princess?"

I gave the king my most reassuring smile. "Well sir, plan B is that we wing it."

At that, it seemed that all those around me wanted to give their opinion on my other plan to deal with the new danger we were all in. Fortunately, all arguments stopped with a roar and announcement from one of our uninvited guests. "SEND OUT THE PRINCESS OR WE WILL BURN OUT ALL YOU VERMIN!"

Once again, you could hear a pin drop in the throne room, but I released my hold on Scom and headed toward the doors while all stood frozen. I could hear the voices of my friends, both old and new, rise in protest as they all came to their senses with my movement. Ro was the first to move and grabbed my arm before I could reach the doors of the throne room. "Where do you think you are going, Princess?"

I looked down at his hand and he slowly released my arm and took a step back into the crowd now gathered around me. "Well you know, Ro, plan B, go see the dragons and figure it out from there."

Scom piped up then in his small voice. "That is not a good plan, Princess, but it is a way to get dead. If you know what I mean, Princess?"

I looked down at my small friend and smiled sadly. "I know it's not the best of plans, Scom, but it's the best plan not to get anyone else dead. If anyone has a better idea, now is the time to speak up or else we go with the plan before us."

No one spoke for a couple of minutes as each of them tried to come up with some plan or excuse for me not to go see our visitors. "Well then, I guess I had better go see what's up with our new friends, before we all become crispy critters, don't you?"

CHAPTER 23

The waves broke against the rocks below the castle walls. The roar of the waves though could not drown out the bellows of the creatures that flew above the castle. As each creature flew down toward the walls, balls of flame and smoke belched out toward the castle and those that stood to defend it. At the highest part of the towers stood a single, small figure, motionless until one of the flying enemies came too close to the castle. With a wave of the figure's hand, the creature was totally engulfed in a bubble of water.

As the creature fell toward the ocean, in a moment of silence, a high eerie laugh could be heard as the bubble hit the water and slowly sank beneath the dark ocean waves taking the trapped creature under the water. All that was left to show where the creature landed was swirl of the waters and a small amount of steam that rose from the spot.

The lone figure looked around once again at the creatures flying around her home and all the damage that they had caused. As the noise increased once again, she whispered to herself, "Oh sister, you were on my list before, but now you and your creatures will pay for what you have done here. Mark my word, little sister, you will pay."

As I walked out the doors to meet the dragons, I could hear my friends scrambling behind me to catch up. Well, even though I didn't want to see anyone else hurt or killed, it was nice not to go see trouble alone.

I had no trouble finding the dragons. All I had to do was follow the sound of the roars and see where all the people were running from. Soon we walked out of the castle into a courtyard with a low wall built around it.

As I looked around, I saw that we were in what was once a small garden hanging off the side of the mountain. In the distance I could see blue sky with small clouds chasing each other in the bright sun. In what had once been a beautiful garden, I could see where the dragons had taken out their impatience. Trees were uprooted and plants were scorched down to the bare ground. Sitting on the walls of the garden, I could see the source of all this destruction and mayhem. Two dragons, one red and a smaller silver one were both looking around the area they had trashed with a satisfied smile on their big lizard faces. This, more than all the damage they had caused, peeved me off more than anything else that had happened so far with these creatures.

Marching out into the garden, I caught the eyes of the two dragons. Each dragon settled down onto the wall as I walked out toward them, looking at me expectantly with their tails twitching like a couple of cats ready to pounce on the mouse they see scurrying across the kitchen floor. Behind me I could hear the others in our group spreading out to cover the dragons with their weapons, but the dragons never took their eyes off of me as I approached them.

As I got within a few feet of the dragons, I reached down and drew out both of my swords. I felt much better with the weapons in my hands, even if I wasn't as familiar with their use as I could have been. Have to remember to get Ro or his brother to give me some lessons with these babies here pretty soon, that is if I survived the next few minutes with the dragons.

Stopping in front of the dragons with both swords in my hands, flashing fire and ice, seemed to unsettle the dragons as I could see them shift their feet and watched as their tails twitched even more as if they were about to launch themselves upon me.

Guess it was time to let them know who was boss around here. "All right, who said you could ruin these gardens like this, and what's up with all the roaring and making such a fuss about?"

To my surprise both dragons grew very still and then bowed their heads and both began to shake and cry. "We are sorry, your highness," whispered the smaller silver dragon. "We did not know that these gardens were yours. We thought that they were your sister's and were only trying to rescue you."

"Yes, your highness," sighed the bigger, red one. "Please forgive us; do not slay us as you have killed the other of us."

I glanced back at my friends with a puzzled look, then back toward the dragons. "You mean that you aren't here to kill me for what I did to Ernie? You're here because you thought I needed to be rescued? Is that what you're telling me?"

A look passed between both dragons, then the silver one whispered again, "Well no, your highness, you wouldn't need to be rescued for here you are."

"Right," the red one said in a louder voice. "We came

more as a backup to help you. Yes, that is right, as the backup to our highness to help here and to help with your other sister."

I gave each of them a look up and down. "Yeah right, backup. Okay now that you see I'm fine you can go back to wherever you guys came from."

Once again a look passed between the two of them and once again the silver dragon spoke. "We cannot do that, your highness, for there is one more of your sisters to deal with and you are our queen now so . . ."

Stomping my foot hard into the ground and holding up my left hand seemed to surprise my two new babysitters, for each sat up with a start and looked down on me with hooded eyes.

Okay, this was just too much for me to take in and I wanted to clear up some things here before we got any further into this conversation. "All right, how about we just stop there for a minute and let me catch up on some things, okay?"

There was that look between them again, but each dragon nodded their agreement. "Okay first off, what are your names and why did you call me your queen?"

The silver dragon, who seemed to be the main speaker between the two, bent down closer to me and whispered, "My name your highness, is Berty, and this one next to me is Regni. Why we call you our queen is because you killed our old king, Ernie, in battle."

I thought for a second and then saw a slight flaw in their reasoning. "Well, yeah, okay I did the deed, but I'm not a dragon, so I can't be your queen, right?"

Both dragons caught their breath as in surprise. "She doesn't know about . . ." Regni blurted out, but was quieted with a quick slash from Berty's tail.

With a quick slash across Berty's nose with my fire

sword, I got her attention back to me and, hopefully, let her know who was boss here. "Okay, enough of that; just tell me what I don't know, and I mean right now."

Regni lowered his head and tucked it away from the reach of my sword, but didn't say a word. Berty, on the other hand, had fire in her eyes, as a drop of blood from the small cut on her face slowly dripped down and landed on the rocks before her.

In the quiet, I could hear the sizzle of her blood as if the liquid was molten and it was burning through the rock and soil it had covered. "Fine, your highness, I will tell you your history. You see for every many, many dragon eggs laid there is one special egg that hatches a demon. This is special because demons are more powerful then plain dragons. For you see, when a demon reaches of age, then they have the ability to take on the shape of us dragons."

Well I guess this puts a bit of a different spin on things, I thought. "So you are telling me that I will turn into a dragon like you guys, right?"

"No, not like us," answered Regni. "You will be a dragon but smaller in size, and you will be able to change at will back and forth from demon to dragon."

Well, okay, so I wouldn't be stuck as a dragon forever, I thought. I didn't think I would look good in green scales anyway. "Okay then you two, how am I more powerful if I'm smaller than you guys?" I asked.

There was that look between the two of them again, then Berty spoke up. "You are more powerful because when you are in our shape you cannot be hurt by dragon fire, your highness."

"Okay, so let me get this all straight here. Dragons are not mad at me because I killed Ernie, your king, right?"

"But, of course not your highness, it is only right since he is the one that killed your father to become king himself," said Regni in a haughty voice who then quickly ducked down as if expecting a blow from Berty, but the silver dragon just gave a slight growl at her companion.

Looking back down at the ground, I took a quick second to reflect on this bit of news, and then realized that I didn't feel quite so bad about killing that big green lizard, Ernie, after all. Both dragons froze like statues as I slowly looked back up at them. Whatever they saw in my eyes seemed to have scared them a bit, for each dragon slowly lowered their head and tail in a gesture of submission.

"And did this dragon king of yours," I asked in a whisper, "kill my father all on his own or was it with someone's help?"

Regni seemed to slink even lower than it seemed possible for the dragon and I could start to detect a slight tremor in the big beast, but Berty seemed to grow bolder. "Your mother is the one that helped Ernie kill your father."

"And you know this how, dragon?" I asked in a low voice.

Maybe it was the tone of my voice or the way my hands were moving those deadly swords around, but Berty didn't seem as confident as she was before, and she looked everywhere around the area except at me. I could see the nervous twitch of her tail start again as her head once again started to lower to the ground.

I turned to the other dragon, figuring I might get an answer from him. "Well Regni, how does she know who killed my father?"

Regni took a quick peek at Berty then at me and whispered, "Well your highness she knows this because she was Ernie's mate and she was there. But she's not the one that did the deed, your highness, so no killing her please, your highness."

I pulled in the urge to once more slash at the silver

dragon, but this time with the ice sword just like I had with the dragon's mate. "Don't worry, Regni, I don't plan on killing her yet, but I still don't see why you guys are here. I'm fine, no trouble and you guys can just take off now, okay? So, so long, bye-bye."

This seemed to perk up the red dragon somewhat, whereas his companion gave me a sly look out of the corner of her eye. I would really have to keep an eye on her, I thought; because I trusted her about as far as I could throw the big lizard, but nether dragon made a move to leave.

"But your highness," whined Regni "you must lead us in the battle, for you are our queen."

"Battle, what battle am I supposed to lead you guys in?"

Regni cocked his head to the side and smiled. "Why the battle with your last sister, Chell, that's what battle, your highness."

"Okay and when is this battle supposed to happen, Regni?"

Regni looked at me with a puzzled look while Berty gave a wicked laugh. "Why your highness, it is not when it is supposed to happen, it is happening right now. That is why we are here to get you."

I looked around at my friends and then back at the two dragons sitting on the wall. "Oh I see, and where is this battle that I'm supposed to be at taking place anyways?"

"Why at your sister's castle, of course," Regni answered now with a touch of impatience in his voice. "So we must hurry so that you can take care of your last sister, as you must, your highness."

Unsure what to do now, I looked back once more at my friends and saw that Ro, his brother, Scom and the king were approaching from where they had all been observing this conversation with the dragons.

I stepped back to meet them to get their take on this turn of events. As we met in the middle of the garden, Scom once again wrapped his arms around my legs as if to anchor me to the spot, but it was Ro who spoke first. "Princess, I don't trust these dragons or their motives," he whispered.

A loud growl came from both dragons and Berty hissed, "This is not for you to comment on shifter, this is dragon business, yes it is."

Well so much for having a private conversation with my friends, guess dragon hearing is better than I thought it was. "Chill out, Berty, these are my friends and I value their opinions."

"Chill your highness, but I am a dragon. I cannot be cold, your highness."

"Just shut up Berty, okay?"

That seemed to quiet the beast down some, but I could also see that it seemed to light a fire in her eyes also. This was one dragon that I needed to never turn my back on.

"Ro is right, Princess," the king whispered. "Dragons are dangerous and unpredictable creatures. Do not trust them."

I looked around at my friends and saw the worry in each of their eyes. "Yes, but is it true what they said about dragons and demons, that I'm one of them?"

No one said a word for a minute and then a small voice piped up from around my leg. "Yes Princess, all that the dragons said is true as far as dragons tells the truth. If you know what I mean, Princess?"

"Well, I guess there is only one thing that I can do then, and that is go with my kind and take care of the last of my sisters, isn't there?" I said as I sheathed both my swords and tried to untangle one small troll from my leg.

Ro reached out and grabbed my arm, but let go as soon

as I looked down at his hand. "Listen, Princess, just let us gather up the army we have here and we will go with you," he said as the others nodded at his advice.

I was tempted to wait, but I felt like this was to the point where this was now my problem and I really didn't want the others there in case something went wrong, as it always seemed to do. I just held out my hand to Ro. "No, you guys stay here, but I would like Mr. Blue, if you don't mind Ro?"

"Why sure, Princess," he said as he handed over my ratty old friend with some reluctance. "I forgot I had him there, in all the excitement."

Tucking Mr. Blue into my belt, I looked down at the small bundle still wrapped around my leg. "Listen Scom you have to stay here and watch over Ro and the other guys, okay?"

He looked up at me with wide, puppy dog eyes and a small tear just gathering at each corner of his eyes. "OH NO, Princess, I will not leave you. I have to go to watch your back with dragons around. If you know what I mean, Princess?"

Oh come on, I thought, really? But I guess it wouldn't hurt to have someone around to watch my back. It's not like I could trust the two dragons waiting on the wall if I got into real trouble. "Fine Scom, but just you and only you can come."

With that the little guy let go of my leg, smiled brightly and all the waterworks went away. Dang, I forgot trolls were known to be great little scammers. Marching over to where the dragons were still sitting, I could see that Berty wasn't too keen on having Scom along for the ride. Well, if she put up too much of a fuss, then I guess there was going to be one less dragon going to my sister's castle.

"Okay we're ready to go, but Regni you will have to give

us a ride, because I have no idea where we are headed, all right with you big guy?"

"Yes, my highness," I would be honored to carry you," he hissed. "But what of the little beasty, it cannot fly."

I just stood there with my hand on my swords and looked at both dragons. A few seconds went by and Berty snorted at her buddy. This seemed to shake him up a little as he quickly glanced at her and then back at me. "Yes sorry, your highness, but I will be happy to carry both of you to your sister's castle," Regni whispered.

Regni hopped down off the wall so that it was easier for Scom and I to climb up onto his back. Once we were settled and secured, I gave a look around at all my unsmiling friends standing around watching us getting ready to leave. Well, I thought, I wasn't really all that happy with the situation either, but there didn't seem to be any way to change it.

With a kick in Regni's side and a quick yell from me, both dragons leaped into the air and soon the castle was far below us. Gods, I really, really hate heights, I thought, as I took a tighter grip onto Regni's back.

CHAPTER 24

Yes, she thought, it is almost done. Two of the ungrateful little brats who banished her to this place were dead. Hopefully this clumsy, stupid clod, Ceri, could get rid of her other sister so that the magic that kept her in this cold dark world would be broken.

She had waited so long to slowly regain her power, and then to steer those three greedy little witches, behind the scenes, to bring their younger sibling back to this world. As each of her daughters was knocked off by Ceri, she could feel the chains of power that held her here slowly dissolve.

As she looked around the world she was imprisoned in, in the distance she could see flashes of lightning and hear the low rumble of an approaching storm. Around her she could sense the scurrying of dark creatures as they hid from the full fury of the onslaught that the storm was bringing.

As the flashes of lightning came closer, they lit up the barren landscape. From her perch high on the hills, she could see the dried bones of some huge, long lost creature scattered among the stunted trees that grew along a slow moving sludge of a river. A cold wind scraped across her skin and whipped her clothes around in the swirl of dust that was kicked up in the turbulence that danced around her.

As she turned away to climb into the hole in the side of the hill that she called home, she thought once again how it would feel to see the sun, to feel the warmth, and not to always live in the cold darkness. That is as long as the stupid beast she had recruited performed as it should. You just never could trust dragons though, so she would really have to keep an eye on the situation, as much as she could from this world.

We flew on through the day, leaving the mountains behind and gliding down into tree covered valleys. As I looked down, I could see the shadows of the dragons chase us across the top of the trees and the open grasslands that we soon came upon. As much as I was afraid of the heights, I did enjoy, somewhat, the feel of the wind as it flowed over us, and its quiet whisper as it talked to us during our travels. The rhythm and movement of Regni's wings, as we leaned down on his body. was hypnotizing.

As the sun was slowly sinking down for the night, I could smell the familiar tangy scent of a large body of salt water. Off in the distance I could see the silver sparkles of light as they reflected off a large band of water.

Finally the dragons started to circle a small grassy valley on one side of a row of low hills. In the gathering darkness on the other side of the hills, just before we landed, I could make out the ocean and what looked like a small island barely off shore.

When Regni's feet touched ground once again, and before I could move a muscle, my quiet little friend, Scom, rolled off his perch in front of me, down the side of Regni and hit the ground with a loud OOMPH sound.

"I really do not like dragons for riding, Princess," Scom,

looking disheveled, shook his head as he looked up at me. "Oh no, I really don't Princess. If you know what I mean?"

"Yeah, I do know what you mean, Scom, I really do," I said as I slid off my ride and stretching my legs that felt numb, and half asleep. As much as I enjoyed the freedom and beauty of the ride, my legs and butt were telling me that dragons were not the softest of all rides.

Berty gave a small, evil chuckle and Regni gave a hurt look at the two of us. "I'm sorry, Princess, but was not the ride to your liking?" whined the bigger dragon.

Looking up, I patted the red guy's nose to comfort him some. "Don't worry about it big guy, I just don't like heights, and you aren't exactly padded in the right spots for such long rides." My words and the quick pat on the nose seemed to pacify the dragon for the moment; so that I could get a quick look around where we had landed.

It was a nice flight and all, even if I don't like heights, but it was really nice to get my feet back on solid ground once again; wherever that ground should be, I thought. Helping Scom up and then looking over at the two dragons once again, I had an uneasy feeling that they had other motives than just bringing me here to help me rid myself of my last sister, but I guess there wasn't much I could do about it right now.

I lit a small fire in the center of our little group to keep the gathering darkness from crowding in on us, and also to keep the chill sea air that flowed over the low hills at bay. Scom moved closer to the fire, rubbing his hands while keeping an eye on the night sky.

"Okay guys, where is this so called castle my sister lives in and where are the other dragons?" I asked, taking hold of the hilts of my swords. "This had better not be a trick or you two will be very sorry."

Once again the dragon, Berty, became the spokesperson

for the two of them. "This is no tricking your highness, you hurt this one's feelings. The castle is just over the hills on the small island just off the shoreline here and the others in our group will soon be here to meet your highness."

"Fine, Berty," I reached down and loosened my ice sword. "Just remember that right now I have a very short temper."

Just then I heard what sounded like the flapping of wings and all around the four of us landed about two dozen dragons. The dragons were of all different colors and sizes and one huge purple beast stood out from the rest because of its two heads that constantly were snapping at each other.

In the night that had fallen, I could make out some of the rest of the dragons, at least the ones that were the closet to us. Looking around I could see two more silver dragons just like Berty as they slid up on each side of her and they started to whisper furiously into her ears. To the right of the trio were a couple of larger green dragons that looked like they came out of a fantasy book from back home. These two just looked Scom and I up and down like we were on the night's dinner menu.

Glancing to my left while keeping an eye on the others, I watched as a beautiful golden dragon slowly walked from the dark into the glow that my small fire gave off, sparkling and shining off his brilliant scales. "Hello, your highness," he whispered as he bowed his head low to the ground. "It is nice to see you again."

I gave him a closer look as he neared me. I could see that he was the smallest of all the dragons that I had seen so far. He was a pure gold, all over, that shone and sparkled in the dancing flames of my small fire, but what really caught my attention was the intelligence and humor that I saw in his eyes.

"Well yes and hello to you," I said with a small curtsy to the polite gold dragon. "And you are who exactly, may I ask?"

"I'm sorry your highness, I had hoped that you would remember me. My name is Nomi," he said with a small, sad smile.

I stood very still for a minute and thought back to when I was little. I could almost grasp a picture of a great golden mound of fun and laughter, but the images seemed to elude me. "I almost remember, but it's all so fuzzy from when I was young. I remember you as being bigger, and your laugh, but I'm sorry I can't seem to . . ."

"That is all right, your highness. At the time you were very young and very small," he gave a chuckle and his smile grew bigger and happier as though remembering better times. "I was your teacher when they brought you to your castle as a baby and watched you grow into a small girl. It is so nice to see what you have grown into now, your highness."

"But I had thought that . . ." I started to say when my attention was attracted by Berty, who was pushing herself to the front of the crowd of dragons.

"Yes, yes that is all nice old home week for you, Nomi, and your highness, but we have more important things to discuss here," Berty hissed as she looked at the gold dragon with an open display of disgust.

I looked at Nomi as he tucked his head down and away from the silver dragon. I walked up to Berty, slowly pulling my ice sword half way from its sheath. "Don't ever interrupt me again when I'm talking to my friends, Berty," I whispered, "or there will be one less dragon in this world, do you understand?"

Berty looked at me and then quickly glanced around her at the other dragons. Seeing no one jump to her defense, the silver dragon once again looked me in the eye and answered me with a slight smirk on her face, "Why yes, your highness, of course. I meant no harm to anyone. It is just that we have so much to consider tonight, your highness."

I stared at Berty 'til she looked away, and then took in her two companions. Each of them also avoided my stare, but each also wore the same sneer on their faces that Berty did. Yeah right, I thought, these three will definitely need to be watched, because I could sense that they were nothing but trouble.

I looked around once again and noticed that all the dragons had come closer to our small group to see what all the action was about.

"Okay so what is your plan for my sister now that I'm here?" I asked the gathered group. No one moved or spoke up and it seemed even the mouthy Berty was quiet, for a change.

"Okay then, what was your plan before I got here?" I asked, but once again the silence in the night was only broken by the crackling of the fire.

"Excuse me Princess, but dragons are not known for their planning; only for their destroying, if you know what I mean, Princess? They are not very bright," squeaked a quiet voice at my side.

I looked down at the little troll whom I had forgotten all about until that second when I heard a rumble to my right. Out of the corner of my eye, I saw both heads of the two-headed dragon reaching down toward Scom.

Without conscious thought, the ice sword was in my hand and swiping to the right, then to the left and finally slashing down the middle. Before the eyes of the stunned dragons, each head fell to the ground, one on each side of Scom and I; the body stood before us, glittering in the fire light like a mountain of glass.

Before any of the dragons could react to my actions, the sword of fire leaped into my other hand and with a few more swipes to each side and down the middle, what once had been a formidable foe became a puddle of water before the gathered group. "No one hurts my friends," I whispered in the quiet.

The silence around the small fire lasted for a few seconds and then the sound of a couple of dozen dragons, minus one (of course), heading for places to hide could be heard in the night.

Soon I was left with three dragons and one frightened troll who was clinging to my legs, standing before the fire. "Well done, your highness, now we will have to gather them all back here all because a troll spoke out," Berty hissed, her dark eyes taking in the small troll lying on the ground and the puddle of water that was once a dragon.

I looked over at Nomi and could see a small smile cross his lips and then quickly disappear. Looking back at Berty, I raised both hands, waving the swords in front of her face. "No one, Berty, and I do mean no one messes with my friends, as I said before; for if they do, they are not long for this world. Now go get them back here before I get really mad, dragon."

Berty could not back up fast enough away from the two swords waving before her face. "Yes, your highness, yes, right away, your highness," she stammered as she and Regni took to the air to find the others.

I could hear a chuckle behind me and knew that Nomi was having fun at the expense of the other dragons. "I see the highness still has a slight temper as she did when she was younger."

"Yes, well seems that being here in this world has added a little edge to my temper," I answered with a little laugh of my own.

Reaching down, I grabbed Scom by his collar and lifted him up and brushed the dirt off of his clothes. "Come on, Scom, the big bad dragons are all gone for now." I laughed as I set him back onto his feet.

The little guy looked around the area, and not seeing any dragons but Nomi, seemed to lessen the fear he had. "Yes well, Princess I guess you showed those dragons," he said as he looked at the rapidly drying puddle that once was a two-headed dragon.

Bending down so that I was eye level with the little troublemaker, I scolded the little guy a little. "Listen Scom, I appreciate your help and ideas, but let's see if we cannot peeve off the big nasties anymore than they already are, okay little guy?"

His eyes got big, but he kept nodding his head as I talked to him. "Oh yes, Princess, I will try very hard." Then he leaned very close to me and whispered, "But Princess, dragons are not very smart. If you know what I mean?"

Nomi laughed even harder than before and almost choked on the troll's reply. "Oh I see your highness that you still have interesting friends around you, oh yes you do."

I stood up and looked at the gold dragon standing before me, and thought that this guy could be a great ally and friend or the most dangerous of the dragons.

I figure no sense beating around the bush with him so I might as well get right to the point of the matter. "Okay Nomi, what's your story and what are you looking for?"

Nomi looked at me closely for a second and then smiled again. "I don't want anything from you, highness. I'm just glad that my student is back and I see that she hasn't forgotten everything that she was taught, is all."

"Oh well, I see I guess, but I am a little confused. I thought that Ernie was my teacher when I was little," I said with some confusion.

Nomi stood up to his full height, which even for being the smallest dragon around was still pretty impressive, and bellowed "I WAS YOUR TEACHER, NOT THAT MURDERING PIECE OF DRAGON DUNG!" After his outburst, he sighed and then slowly inched back to the ground. "Sorry your highness, you were my charge and my favorite student."

I looked at Nomi and could see a large tear drop from his eye. Feeling sorry for him, I walked over and patted him on his rough nose. "It's all right Nomi; it's just so hard to know who to trust in this world. It seems that everyone has wanted something from me since I have gotten here. Even my friends want something, even though it is a good thing, but they still want something, and all I want is to go home."

Giving me a long, sorrowful look Nomi nodded his head as I let loose my own little pity party. Once I was done, he reached over and rubbed his nose against me just as my foster parent's cat had done when I was sad. "I understand, your highness, that you miss your other home, but really this is where you were born and all and it really is your home," the dragon said in an understanding voice.

Feeling a pull on my clothes, I looked down at Scom who was eagerly dancing in place while trying to get my attention. "Yes Scom, what is it now?"

"Princess, I think you should listen to this dragon. I think that this dragon is a not so dumb dragon as the rest of them. If you know what I mean, Princess?"

I looked at Scom then back to Nomi, and then back to Scom again. "You know, I do know what you mean, Scom, and I think you're right, little guy, this is a not dumb dragon, and one I think we can trust."

Nomi huffed a little in annoyance then gave a little laugh. "Yeah I guess I will take that as a compliment little troll, even the not so dumb part. But know this, highness, even though the others are not the smartest creatures, they are very conniving creatures, so watch your back at all times."

"Don't worry Nomi, I think after being in this world for awhile I can take care of myself pretty well."

Nomi looked at the spot on the ground that was just barely damp where the two-headed dragon had stood and chuckled again. "Yes I see what you mean, your highness, but remember you caught them by surprise this time. Next time you may not be so lucky."

Scom and I looked where Nomi's eyes lingered and I agreed with him. "Yeah I see what you mean, big guy."

Just then I heard the sounds of some of the returning dragons in the air. Out of the dark walked both Berty and Regni. Regni had a hang dog look on his face and Berty's looked like the cat that ate the canary.

Looking at both of the dragons I figure whatever news that they had probably wasn't going to be good. "Well guys, where are the other dragons? Are they on their way here?"

Berty's smile only increased and Regni seemed to slump even lower to the ground. "I'm sorry your highness, but the others feel that you are not a true queen since you took the side of the troll over one of your own. So they will no longer help you with your sister, your highness," Berty hissed with delight.

I looked around at the little group that was still gathered around the fire then back toward the low hills that hid my sister's castle. "Fine then, I guess I take care of her myself."

A small cough drew my attention back to Nomi who

had a worried look on his face. "That is fine your highness, but remember that this is the last of your sisters and the only one in this world that can send you back home."

The big guy's got a point, I thought. "Yeah you are right, Nomi, let's just hope she isn't as crazy as the other two were, right?"

Since the looks on the other faces wasn't very encouraging, I figured that it would be a long day tomorrow. "Look everyone, how about we bed down for the night and take tomorrow as it comes, okay?"

Everyone just quietly nodded and headed off toward an area to find a bed while Scom and I lay down by the dying embers of my fire. My last thought before sleep took me was that it would be nice if tomorrow I could finally find a way home. Yeah, yeah, I know, it hasn't happened yet, but what the heck, a girl has to have some hope.

CHAPTER 25

Rolling over, the first morning light danced across my eyelids, bringing me up from my deep slumber. Though it was the loud snorts and snoring of the nearby sleeping dragons that finally made me decide it was time to get up and get the day going.

I sat up and looked at my big fuzzy, and might I say lumpy, pillow slash night guard, Mr. Blue. He gave me a face full of teeth grin that would scare a great white, if there were any around in this world, and as he stretched out, he let go a loud burp and accompanying other body noises that would wake the dead (if the smell didn't kill them). Just gross!

Scrambling up and out of the deadly zone of his smell, I couldn't help but laugh at the hurt look on the big demon's face. "Sorry, big guy, but a girl has to have some standards and that is just rude, dude." I laughed as he grinned back at me and let rip more bodily noises with satisfaction. Yeah, I think I need to find out what Ro had been feeding him while he was watching my best friend, because whatever it was was going to be off his diet or I would have to find another pillow.

I looked around at the others as they slept and tried to

figure out what I was going to do today. I knew that I needed to go see my sister sooner or later but, without the other dragons to back me up, I wasn't really confidant about how that visit would turn out.

I turned and stretched and could hear the popping of Mr. Blue's bones and muscles as he did the same. I was glad that with a snap of my fingers I had brought the guy back from being a ratty old teddy bear to my demon protector. Especially since it seemed to tee off old Berty a bit to see Mr. Blue in all his size and glory, but I also thought it might be a good idea to have another ally to watch my back in unknown territory while we slept.

What was funny was how Mr. Blue and Nomi greeted each other as long lost friends, but it did make me feel a little better about trusting my old tutor. As I watched Mr. Blue bend over to pick up a large, nasty looking insect that happened to be slithering by, I heard one more large release of his nauseating gas from the south end of his big body. Unfortunately for Berty and Regni, that end was pointed directly at them.

As the big guy stood up and crunched on his newly discovered wiggly breakfast (grosser still), I watched as the noses on each of the dragons twitched and jerked, and I could swear I saw tears leak from their eyes as each dragon jumped up from their resting place and were desperately looking around for the source of the rancid smell. I almost felt sorry for the two, but remembered how rude the silver dragon had been yesterday and that feeling soon vanished.

Both Scom and Nomi sat up and looked around at the two retching dragons, wondering what their problem was. Mr. Blue's grin was even bigger than before which led me to think that that last little release of his deadly gas may not have been an accident after all. Oh well, enough fun and games for the morning, time to get going with the day's adventures.

Scom and I found some of those strange trees, which had the chocolate tasting apples, a little way from camp and a small pool of clear water so we soon had a hearty breakfast. The dragons, on the other hand, were not so happy with our choice of breakfast and disappeared for awhile to hunt for their own meal while Mr. Blue found some more wiggly crawly things to munch down on.

Nomi was the first of the dragons back from breakfast and we sat down and talked about what I should do when visiting my sister, and exactly where her castle was. Scom sat quietly by without saying much, but I could tell that he wasn't very happy with what Nomi had to say.

I found out that there were two sets of low hills and a small shallow valley that had to be crossed to reach my sister's castle. Once I got through this area, all I had to do was follow the path out onto a land bridge that led to the castle itself. Sounded simple enough to me, but so far nothing in this world had been that simple, I thought.

Soon the other two returned from their breakfast trip and we settled on a plan; or at least a concept of a plan, well okay, really just an idea. It was that Scom, Mr. Blue and I would travel to my sister's castle and try to reason with her while the others tried to talk the reluctant dragons into coming back to help their queen. Yeah, I know, fat chance that was going to probably happen the way my luck in this world was going, I thought.

Later in the afternoon, after a quick lunch, I watched as the three dragons flew off on their mission. Scom, Mr. Blue and I headed up a path that Nomi told me would take us to the castle's front door. As we trudged up the slope to the small hills, I had hopes that at least Nomi would be able to talk some, if not all, the dragons into coming back. As for Regni and Berty, I didn't really trust the two of them to help me; the thought was at the back of my mind that they would be more likely to help my enemies.

After a couple of hours of walking, we hit a rocky area on our path and from where we were I could see the top of the pass that we would soon come to. I called a halt and plopped my butt down on one of the bigger rocks to take a load off of my aching feet.

I was lost in thought about how nice it would be if my two companions had wings like me. It would save some wear and tear on my feet if we could all just buzz over these hills. Of course, now that I think about it, the dragons could have also just dropped us off at the front door of the castle too and saved us all some shoe leather.

A low growl from the big guy and Scom's words drew me back to our present situation. "Umm, Princess, I think we may have visitors. If you know what I mean?"

I looked up at Scom and patted Mr. Blue, who a second ago, had been sitting on the ground besides me, but was now up and searching the surrounding rocks. This seemed to calm him down a bit, but he was still growling low in his chest, so that only I could hear the sound.

As I stood up, I looked around to see if maybe it was the dragons that had returned. I figured Berty would love the chance to get a good scare into me for payback because of that little scratch I left on her nose.

"Who's out there?" I questioned the surrounding rocks. "Is that Berty, because if it is, I am so not amused."

Scom took a sniff in the air then looked at me with some fright on his face. "It smells like fish, Princess, not of dragons. If you know what I mean?"

That's when I caught a whiff of whatever it was too. He was right; it smelled like old fish mixed with seaweed. Just then, a small bunch of little creatures stood up from behind the rocks.

They were small little guys about four feet high and grey in color with no necks between their bodies and their heads. They had long, thin arms and legs with small webbed hands and feet to match their stature. Their faces looked odd in that they had no noses, small little mouths and their eyes were huge bulging black bubbles that took up most of their faces.

What they lacked in size was made up for in the long, very wicked, tipped tridents that each creature held. We all stood around staring at each other for a few minutes when one of the creatures, that wore a large shell necklace, stepped forward and addressed me.

"Princess, we are your guide," it whispered as if its tiny mouth could not produce any noise louder. "Our highness has sent us here to make sure that you make it back to our home." With that speech all the creatures bowed to me and then just stood there looking expectant.

"Okay and if I don't want your guidance?" I said looking around at the speaker as more of the creatures emerged from the rocks.

No one said anything for a second then slowly all thirty or forty of the creatures that were around us raised their weapons toward us. "Oh I see," I said as I looked around, "guide us, oh yes, I do see what you mean. Well why don't you just lead on then?"

Scom looked around at all the creatures, then back to me. "Umm yes, Princess, I think that would be a wise move. If you know what I mean?"

Looking around once again at the crowd we seemed to have attracted as he put his hand in mine, I smiled at the little guy to reassure him. "Yeah, Scom, believe me, I do know what you mean. Discretion is better in this case, besides they are taking us in the right direction so we follow them for now."

She looked into the cloud of smoke that issued from the fire in front of her, slowly blinking as the images flowed in front of her bright, mad eyes. Outside, the storm that had earlier raged across the land was dying its last breath. The winds blowing through the scoured bones of those that were not as quick as others to find shelter.

"Well, well," she mumbled to herself, "the little brat is on her way to her little family reunion; how interesting that will be."

She lets out a small cackle, startling herself. She looks around the small enclosure's shadows for the source of the sound then turns her eyes back toward the fire still showing ever changing images from a world she once ruled.

Looking deep in the fire, she thinks back to the dragon that was killed yesterday by her youngest. Yes, she thinks, it is time to reconsider keeping Ceri around after she is done being so useful. She thinks just how powerful the little girl has grown; yes, maybe she should contact the one that will take care of her for good, but after, yes after she has served her mother once more.

We were back to using up good shoe leather once again. After meeting our guides, we traversed the pass in the hills and were now headed down into a small, dry, thin valley. I could see that the floor of the valley was only a couple of hundred feet or so across before it climbed back up to the next set of hills; but the walls were very close together in some parts and were at least twenty feet high.

The little guys that were our guides seemed to be a bit more nervous as we started down the path, but I couldn't see any problems or any place that anyone could hide since the whole area was so bare. The only thing I could see on the floor of the valley was what looked like small piles of sticks and little rocks.

Before we reached the bottom of the path leading into the valley, the whole group stopped and the little guy with the shell necklace came back to where we were standing. Looking worried, like the rest of his people, he was starting to make me a little jumpy.

"Princess," he whispered in a voice so low that I had to strain to hear him at all, "we must insist that you be very quiet while we cross the valley."

"Why?" I whispered back, bending over to get closer to the little guy while glancing all around for some sign of danger. "I don't see any problems or threats," I said as I stood up and raised my voice.

"Please, just do as I say, Princess," he said in an even a lower whisper.

"Fine, whatever," I whispered right back at him, giving Scom and Mr. Blue a shrug and confused look.

We started to cross the little valley when I felt a sneeze come on from all the dust that was being kicked up from so many feet marching across the dry, sandy floor.

I let out a small sneeze that seemed to echo and bounce off the walls of the small valley. All of a sudden two things happened and I realized why we should be very quiet in this place. All the creatures around us froze in place and as one they looked at me with large, frightened, reproachful eyes. As I shrugged my shoulders, the last echoes of my sneeze returned from down the small valley and died as I whispered, "Sorry!"

As I finished my apology, it seemed to start a panic for the little guys for we were all suddenly scrambling toward the other side of the valley. Behind me, I heard a scream that suddenly was cut off in mid sound. Before I could look behind me to see what had happened, a small patch in the wall sprang open and what looked like a bug from hell reached out and grabbed one of the small creatures in front of me. Before this guy could so much as make a sound, he was pulled into the hole and the patch of wall closed over his fate. The only thing I could hear as we passed the spot was a very loud crunching sound coming from the lair of the bug.

As my feet hit the path leading back up to the next set of hills, I turned to see that Scom was still running across the valley. I saw the little troll dodging back and forth between the bugs that were reaching out of their holes as they grabbed for the moving smorgasbord that was now crossing their path.

I started to dart out to help Scom when I felt a pair of huge hands grab me and toss me further up the path. Before I hit the ground on my butt, Mr. Blue was down the path and had grabbed Scom and was running straight back up to where the rest of the survivors waited. I ran down to the edge of the path where Mr. Blue set Scom down and slowly smiled at me like a puppy that had just fetched his favorite toy for his master.

Looking up at the big guy and checking over the little troll for any missing parts, I failed to notice the very large hole that opened in the side of the hill behind Mr. Blue. The biggest bug of all grabbed the demon around the center of his body and disappeared into its hole before anyone could move.

I stood in shock for what seemed like forever before I lunged, screaming toward the hole that my best friend had just disappeared into. Before I could get very far though, I was tackled from behind and all I could do was lie on the ground and listen to the loud crunching sound that came from the hole in the wall.

Soon the sound stopped and I pushed off the creatures that had been holding me down. Through my tears, I watched as the door to the bug's home slowly started to open. I flicked my wrist and started a small ball of flame in my hand, vowing that I would give the thing that had made a meal of Mr. Blue the biggest case of heartburn it had ever had.

As I watched the hole and built the flame higher, I saw the cover to the hole go flying across the valley and hit the other side slamming into another bug that had taken that second to reach out of its hole. The dirt door smeared the bug all over the wall with a loud crunching sound and splat from bug guts being smeared all over.

Looking back at the other bug hole that Mr. Blue disappeared in, I was astounded to see that it wasn't the bug that was coming out of the hole, but my big fuzzy companion. Mr. Blue just stood in the middle of the path and grinned up at me with his silly look. As he calmly walked up toward our little group, I could see him wipe his paw across his mouth and just as he stepped up to us, he let out a loud belch that echoed down through the valley. With that sound echoing off the walls, all the other holes across the valley suddenly shut; hiding the horrors within them.

Looking around, I could see that only five of our guides were left from the group that had started across the valley floor. I checked down in the valley to see if anyone else was still there, but the only movement I saw were small bones slowly slipping from the holes of the bugs in the valley. Guess those weren't twigs I saw on the floor of the valley after all. Gods, this world was so dangerous and gross sometimes, I thought.

I turned back to get our guides to carry on with the hike to my sister's castle, but saw that Scom, Mr. Blue, and I were all by our lonesome. Seems that our guides felt it wasn't too healthy to hang out with us anymore and we were on our own finding the way to my sister. Well, I guess, I couldn't blame the little guys too much. I just hoped my sister wouldn't be too peeved at me for losing so many of her guides, or guards or whatever they were.

Looking at the other two, I shrugged my shoulders and started up the path to the next hills. "Let's go guys, we're burning daylight."

They both looked at me strangely for a second before Scom quickly looked around in alarm and then asked, "But Princess, I don't see anything burning; if you know what I mean? I mean it is hot out, I guess, but…"

I laughed at the troll who was so literal sometimes that I forgot that he didn't always get my meaning. "Don't worry about it. Let's just get moving, okay?" I smiled to put the two of them at ease while we headed, hopefully, to a meeting that would soon send me home.

"Oh, Princess, okay," Scom answered while Mr. Blue just gave a small little burp and plastered that silly grin of his back on his face.

CHAPTER 26

The two dragons slowly circled the clearing in the trees that was nestled in the large valley, looking down to see if any of their companions had arrived before them. The darkness was complete with the moon hidden behind the rolling clouds. The eternal whisper of the wind through the silver leaves twinkling on the trees could hide the noise made by an army of dragons.

Slowly the dragons landed, one to each side of the clearing, looking around alertly for any sign of danger. After several minutes of waiting, they came together in the middle of the clearing. "Well I think we are the first ones here," the smaller silver dragon said looking over her shoulder and then into the night sky.

"Yes, you are right Berty," the other bigger red dragon sighed. "I guess we should be safe enough here until the others come."

"Sorry Regni, I guess I'm still a little nervous ever since we met the queen," Berty said as she settled down onto the ground and relaxed her guard. "Who would have thought that such a little slip of a girl could take down someone as powerful as my mate, Ernie?"

"Yes and she didn't do so badly against Nil either when

he tried to eat that troll of hers last night either."

"Umm well I guess her half demon and witch blood does give her an advantage over us dragons," Berty whined, thinking only now of the trouble that the new queen would cause if all the other dragons decided to follow after her.

Regni walked closer to the smaller dragon while taking a last look around the clearing and at the sky above them. "Yes well when the others hear that she has killed another one of us for no reason I'm sure that the dragons will band together to finally destroy the mad queen."

"Third dragon killed, but what dragon is tha . . ."

With a swish the unsaid words were replaced by the sounds of blood hitting the ground and the gurgling coming from the silver dragon; Regni laughed and backed up from the astounded Berty as she felt her life's blood pouring through the claws that she held up to her newly torn throat.

"Why, you are the third dragon Berty," Regni laughed again. "It's just too bad that I could not get here in time, before the queen slashed you with her blades."

Berty slide down to the ground and tried to speak, but nothing came out of her torn throat except the sound of escaping air. All too soon the blackness took her to see her mate on the other side.

Regni burned the still body erasing all trace of how Berty had died. Looking into the fire, he saw the ghostly figure of his true queen and cocked his head as if listening to some silent commands. "Yes, your highness, she will die after she takes care of her sister – just as you wish."

As the flames died down, Regni took flight to where the real meeting of the dragons was to take place. It was really too bad that he would be bringing such bad news about Berty and the mad little queen to the rest of the dragons, he thought.

As the red dragon flew higher into the air he failed to notice the shadow that crept from out of the trees where he had been hiding. As the creature slowly walked over to Berty's remains, the moon peeked out from behind the clouds and glinted off golden scales; the creature silently and sadly looked down at what was left of Berty for several minutes before taking flight and following Regni's path to the meeting of the dragons.

The sun of the new morning woke me and I rolled over and looked down from the top of the pass that we had laid up in last night. Scom and I figured that it would be smarter to finish our trip to my sister's castle in the morning rather than in the dark.

From where we sat, I could see that the path led down the side of this hill then across a thin bridge and up to the castle walls. Nudging Scom with my foot, he turned over and mumbled in his sleep. "Come on sleepy head, up and at them," I said as I gently nudged the troll again.

Slowly the troll sat up and looked around the area and then down at the castle. "I'm up Princess. What's for breakfast?" the troll said as he stretched and stood up from his sleeping spot.

I looked down at Scom and then around the bare clearing we had spent the night in and thought breakfast did sound good right about now, but that wasn't going to happen this morning.

A loud crunching noise came from where Mr. Blue was sitting and we both looked over to where the big guy was standing. He had lifted up a large boulder and was stuffing paws full of wiggly things into his mouth. Turning away so that I wouldn't catch sight of exactly what he was eating, I caught Scom's eyes and laughed at the look on his face.

"Well you can have some of what he is having," I chuckled and pointed to Mr. Blue, "but other than that there isn't much for us to eat around here, little guy."

I had to laugh as Scom turned very pale when he quickly looked at the big demon and then back at me. "Umm yeah that's okay I'm not all that hungry. If you know what I mean, Princess?"

Hearing more crunching behind me, I nodded at the troll. "Yeah, believe me, I do know what you mean, Scom."

I heard the rock drop and the crunching stop and turned to see Mr. Blue walking toward us with a big grin plastered all over his face.

"Well, are you done with your meal, big guy?" I asked

He just let out a small burp in response and patted his full extended belly. Well at least one of us had had a good last meal before we headed down into the lion's den, I thought. "Okay let's go guys. There's no sense in keeping my sister waiting any longer then we have to." With that the three of us headed down the path to the castle, and whatever lay in wait for us there.

We reached the castle's bridge by the sea about noon. Our walk was almost as boring as the landscape around us. Once we came off the path from the hills and, as I looked around the flat plains before the castle, on each side of us there was nothing but grey, dull flatness. No trees, crops, or villages. I begin to wonder where the people lived that my sister had sent as our guides, but saw no sign of life anywhere on this land.

As we stood at the edge of the bridge, I got a better look at where my sister lived. The castle was built as if the walls rose right out of the sea. Expecting a dark and forbidding building, I was surprised at the many colors that abounded in the castle. It was almost as if the fortress wasn't built of rock, but of colorful coral like I had seen back home.

Walking across the bridge, we could see into the clear water close to the land. In the water we saw movement in between what looked like small buildings that were as colorful as the castle itself. Stopping to watch, I could see that the flashes of movement in the water were from people who looked a lot like those that had guided us yesterday. Well I guess that explains why I thought that they had looked and smelled like fish, I guess.

I was brought back from my daydreaming when Scom started to tap me on my leg, which became very annoying quickly as each tap was harder than the first. "Umm Princess, I think you need to look at this."

Looking up and to where the troll was pointing, I forgot all about the people in the water and concentrated on the ones that were now coming from the castle. These creatures were very different from the little ones that we had met yesterday.

There were five of the creatures in the group. Each one was almost as tall as Mr. Blue with blue-grey, rough looking skin and dark lidless eyes that were way set off on the side of their heads. Their bodies were more muscular than the ones we had met yesterday and, as the group stopped before us, each of them smiled, showing a row of teeth that would have given Mr. Blue a run for his money. They almost reminded me of pictures I had seen of the hammerhead shark back in my own world.

We stood there for a few minutes, both groups just looking at each other until the foremost one in the group turned and pointed at us then, with a grunt, back toward the castle then turned back to look at me.

I turned and looked at the other two in my group. Scom

just shrugged his shoulders while Mr. Blue looked at me and grunted. I looked back at who I took was the leader and smiled. "You want us to go with you?"

The same creature just pointed at us again, grunted and pointed back at the castle then just stood there with his arms crossed over his chest.

I smiled at the group standing before us. I looked for weapons, but saw nothing like what the little guys had on them. "And if we don't want to go with you, then what?" I asked as I sized them up.

None of the creatures said a word, but they all straightened up and each of their smiles grew larger, showing off five sets of nasty choppers. Yeah I had seen that look and smile before from Mr. Blue just before he devoured his next meal. Guess we were going to the castle with our escorts after all.

"Lead on," I said as I pointed toward the castle.

The creatures hesitated for a second then frowned, almost as if they were disappointed in missing a meal; but then, as a group, they turned and walked toward the castle's door with us following close behind them.

The door of the castle looked dark and like it was moving, but as we got closer to it I could see that it was a sheet of constantly moving water flowing down the entrance. As we walked through the water, the cool sting on my cuts and smell told me that they water came from the sea somehow.

Coming out from under the water, I stopped as I took in the inside of my sister's home. We were in a large cavern-like room that was open to the sea in the middle of the floor. In fact, the open area took up most of the floor area with a small ledge running around the walls. Steps lead down into the open water and, as I looked down, I could see what looked like caves carved into the walls in the water. Since I could see creatures popping in and out of these caves, I figured that these must be their homes, offices or such. Looking up, I could see steps that lead up to some more caves carved into the rock, but also noticed that these had barred doors over them.

"Hello sweet little sister of mine." I heard from across the open floor.

I stopped sightseeing and looked across the open water and saw a set of stairs leading up to a throne that my sister was sitting on. What is it with these girls and the high seats? Really they all sit up above everyone and looked down at the world like they owned it. No wonder the three of them were bat poop crazy, I thought.

We slowly walked around the edge of the wall to get closer to my sister. "Hello back, sis," I replied as we and our guards came to the bottom of the steps. Looking up at her, all I could think that boy this sure did feel like I had been in this situation before.

My sister slowly stood and gave me a little nod. "My name is Chell, sister, and I have been waiting for you to arrive at my little home," as she slowly smiled and spread her arms out to encompass her castle.

Looking up at her, I could see that, like my other sisters before her, she was short and thin in stature. Her hair was as green as seaweed and hung down in long strings as if she had just stepped out of the shower. As she walked down the stairs and came closer to me, I saw that her eyes were a deep, dark blue and her skin was a light grey color like the rest of her people.

"Hello Chell, I'm Ceri, glad to finally meet you again," I said.

Chell just stopped about three steps above us and just out of my arms reach. Guess my ability to take my sisters' powers preceded me. "So where are your other pets, the dragons?" she asked as she took in my two companions, her eyes lighting up in anger.

Not liking where these conversation was starting to head, I tried to explain what had happened and that I didn't know that the dragons would attack her. Heck, I didn't even know that I was the dragon's queen until a couple of days ago.

The anger shimmered in her eyes for awhile as I told her about Ernie and the other dragons and the problems I had had with them. She laughed when I told her what I had done with the two-headed dragon and how all the others had flown away in fright.

"You know, Ceri, I would have loved to have been there to see that sight," she said with cheer in her voice. "Okay, so they aren't your dragons; so what should I do with you now that you are here, little sister?"

As I looked at Chell, I thought that maybe I had one sister that was sane and she would send me back home without any problems. A girl can always hope you know. "I just want to go home is all, Chell. I didn't come here to cause trouble. In fact I never even knew this world existed until a little while ago."

Chell stood there looking me in the eyes for awhile then she gave me a warm smile and came down to stand before me. "Okay sister, I believe you and I will send you home."

"Umm just like that?" I asked surprised that I was finally getting what I had been after since the first day I landed on this world. "You're not going to get me for getting rid of the others or any of that stuff, just tap your heels three times and here you go – back home?"

Chell looked at me, puzzled and then shook her head, smiling at me. "I think that all that happened was not all our sisters' fault. I think that there was someone behind them pushing them and putting ideas into their heads."

"And you, my sister?" I asked.

"I had not talked to the other two since we banished our mother together and you were sent to the other world," she said. "I keep to myself and take care of my own kingdom."

"Okay, so you aren't bat poop crazy after all. Nice to know, big sis," I said as I finally felt some hope in that I would soon be home in my own bed.

"All right, Ceri, we will go to my library and find the spell that will send you home," my sister said as we walked toward the steps leading up to the barred caves.

As her first foot hit the bottom steps leading upward, our little guide with the shell necklace from the other day came running into the room shouting for my sister. "MY PRINCESS, THE DRAGONS ARE BACK AND ATTACKING . . . !" Unfortunately, his yells were cut off by a ball of flame that shot through the doorway and fried the little guy to a crisp.

She looked into the smoke as the dragons attacked her daughter's castle. Hopefully this would get the results she wanted or there was going to be some roasted dragons when she got back to her world.

Soon, yes, very soon, she could feel it in her bones that she would be home and in charge once again. Then all that had opposed her would feel her wrath. When she had once again conquered this world, she would go back to the true home that she had been banished from and then the real payback would begin.

"YOU HAVE LIED TO ME, CERI!" my sister yelled as she turned on me, her eyes flashing. "Your pets have killed my people, again."

"Wait, no, you don't understand. I didn't lie, really. I just want to go home, Chell," I cried as I heard the roar of the dragons and felt the heat from their flames through the castle walls. "Just let me go talk to them, I'll stop them; really I will."

The fire in her eyes flashed even brighter as she looked down at the pile of ash that was once one of her subjects, then back at me. "One of yours for one of mine," she whispered as a she whipped her hands in the air and a ball of water suddenly engulfed Mr. Blue.

"PLEASE NO!" I yelled as I saw the big guy struggling in the giant water bubble as he tried desperately to get air that wasn't there anymore. That's it, I thought, as I lunged and grabbed hold of my sister's arms; I'm tired of you guys hurting my friends.

My sister struggled in my arms until, like the others, her power was transferred to me and she disappeared into nothing. I heard the huge bubble behind me fall to the ground and was deluged with a wave of water.

Looking around, I saw that Mr. Blue was lying on the ground soaking wet, but his chest was slowly rising and falling as he took in air. Scom had a trident in each hand and was holding the guards back away from where I was standing.

The creatures looked where their queen had once stood and then at the ceiling of the castle where we could all still hear the roar of the dragons. As one, they turned and dived into the opening of the floor, soon disappearing into the sea and leaving the three of us alone in the castle.

Slowly I sank down onto the steps, thinking that I had been so close to going home. I felt the powers of my last sister flowing through me to settle in a mark on my arm, but I didn't really care at that moment. Nothing had been more important to me than getting out of this world and back to my own home; now all that was gone because of some stupid dragons.

Sitting there on the steps, I noticed that the roaring of the dragons had died down, and that I could hear a voice calling to me from outside. "Oh your highnesses, come out to play with us."

I couldn't tell who was talking, but I just knew it had to be Berty. Only she would have the gall to pull off a stunt like this. Well, I thought, as I stood and drew both swords; there was going to be one dragon that was going to meet her mate very soon and in person. As I walked toward the outside and the dragons, I could feel a rage that I had never felt before grow inside me.

"Umm, Princess, where are you going please?" Scom asked as he stepped in front of me.

I just stood and looked down at the little troll. His eyes grew big and he stepped back, but kept talking to me even though his voice was quieter than before. "Please, Princess, this is a trap. They want you to go out there and get killed. If you know what I mean, Princess?"

"Don't worry, Scom. I do know exactly what you mean and before they take me down, I will kill one silver dragon," I said as I walked toward the door. I heard a grunt and saw out of the corner of my eye Mr. Blue getting up and shaking himself off from his bubble bath.

I stopped and watched as he walked over to me and grinned. "You don't have to come with me, big guy. I can handle this on my own."

Mr. Blue just shook his head and I got showered in water. He just looked at me again and started to shuffle toward the door. Okay, I thought, I guess we go together.

As we hit the door and walked out on the bridge, I was glad that he was with me for I could see that there were a dozen dragons waiting for me on the other side of the bridge.

No one made a sound until we hit the end of the bridge and stepped onto solid ground. I looked around for the one dragon that I really wanted but only saw one dragon I knew. "Why, hello, your highness," Regni sneered.

I looked around once more at the group and finally caught sight of Nomi toward the back of the group. Looking at the red dragon, Regni, I asked, "Okay where is she? Where is that silver demon?"

"Why, your highness, who could you mean?" Regni sneered again.

I looked around again for the silver dragon who was the cause of all my troubles; wondering why she wasn't at the front of the group, and thinking that Regni's attitude was really starting to peeve me off.

Fine, I thought, since Berty wouldn't show herself, I guess that I would have to deal first with Regni then go looking for the sliver dragon. "I'm looking for Berty, Regni, and I'm running out of patience with you," I said as I stepped closer to the red dragon.

This seemed to wipe the sneer off his face, especially when I raised both swords and waved them under his big red snout. He took a few steps back. Looking at the other dragons around him then back at me he said, with some of the sneer returning to his voice, "Oh come now, you know where Berty is since you are the one that killed her, your highness."

I looked at Regni and then at the others standing around trying to figure what they were talking about. "Umm, Regni, I don't know what game you're playing, but I am starting to get really peeved with it. Now you had better explain . . ."

"Explain what, daughter?" I heard a strange voice say behind me.

I slowly turned and looked at the tall, thin, grey-haired lady standing at the edge of the bridge we had just crossed. The one thing that really stood out on the lady was her eyes. They were a dark green, but they had this glimmer in them as if they saw something that only they could see. You know sort of like a glimmer of madness.

"And what do you mean daughter, lady? My mother was banished from this world by my sisters," I said as I looked this old crazy bat over from head to toe, trying to figure out what her and Regni's game was.

She just smiled at me and crossed over the bridge and walked so that she was standing in front of the dragons. She turned back to face me with a smile on her face that would curdle milk. Oh yeah, I thought, my sisters may have been bat poop crazy but they had nothing on this old gal.

"You're right," she whispered. "Your sisters did banish me to a very dark and cold world, but you see, Ceri, without them around anymore, I was able to break their spell and, well, here I am. Surprise!"

Oh, this was so not going to end good for me, I thought. "Okay, so what do you want? I guess you want me dead too, mother dear?" Yeah I know I was pressing my luck, but I didn't think I was going to live out the day anyway so I might as well go for broke.

My mother just sort of looked at me and her smile faded. "Well I was thinking of killing you, especially since you went and killed Berty and all." The dragons growled their agreement at her choice of words but went silent as she held up her hand. "But I think I have a better plan for you, my little one."

"Look, let's get this straight. I didn't kill Berty." Not that she didn't deserve it, I thought. "So how about you just go back to where you came from and let me be," I said as my mother smiled that crazy-looking smile I had seen earlier.

"But my little one, I'm here to give you exactly what it is you have wanted all this time." Before I could move, I saw a flick of my mother's hand and Mr. Blue and I were engulfed in a cloud of blackness.

I fell on top of Mr. Blue and as the darkness reeled me down into its icy pit, I thought I heard Scom scream my name. My last thought was that I hoped that I woke up from whatever that rag had done to me.

Slowly the black cloud dissipated as Scom, the dragons and Queen Ellie looked at the spot where two demons had once been. The silence dragged on for several seconds before the dragons roared their approval and Scom sank down to his knees with tears in his eyes. "What have you done, your highness?"

The queen laughed at the little troll. "Oh don't worry, I just gave her wish and sent her back home is all."

This quieted the dragons and one large black dragon stepped forward with a roar. "WHAT DO YOU MEAN SENT HER HOME? SHE WAS SUS . . ."

Quick as a flash, Queen Ellie turned, flicked her wrist and the dragon burst into a mountain of flame and then a pile of ash. "Does anyone else have an opinion about what I did with Ceri?" she asked as she looked at all the dragons standing around the clearing. There was neither sound nor movement. "Yeah that's what I thought."

Slowly she stretched out her arms toward the warm sun, turning in a circle as everyone nervously watched her. Turning back toward the dragons she gave her orders to Regni and the others. "You dragons are to fly to all the kingdoms, tell them that all my daughters are gone and that I am back. They are to send representatives to my castle in one month. Tell them that if they don't show that the old penalties will be enforced," she said as she pointed to the pile of ash lying on the ground.

"Now go, all of you, except you, Regni," the queen ordered as she waved her arms, shooing the dragons into the air like a flock of birds.

Regni slid up next to the queen and bowed his head. "And what would my true queen have from her humble servant, Regni, your highness?"

Queen Ellie looked over the red dragon and smiled. "First quit with the butt kissing and listen good, dragon. I'm going to set a bounty on my daughter's head, I want you to go back to her world and spread the news."

The red dragon looked worried, but a quick glance at the pile of ashes kept him silent.

"You do know that all kinds of creatures have been banished to her world, right?"

"Yes, your highness," Regni whispered.

"Good, then let all creatures know that there is a bounty on Ceri's head and the first one to kill my little one will have a free ride home and my undying gratitude," the queen said as she reached up and petted Regni on the nose. "Do not fail me, dragon; for you know the punishment," she said as she grasped his nose and turned it toward the pile of ash that was blowing away in the wind.

"Oh no, your highness, I will never fail you," Regni called as he quickly took flight toward a portal between worlds that only the dragons and the queen knew about.

Ellie looked after the dragon then smiled to herself. "Oh yes, dragon, you had better not fail me." Then she turned and walked into the gathering darkness.

Scom sat silently on the bridge, ignored by all the others. He knew that he had to protect his Princess. Trying to think what to do, the little troll stood up and watched where Queen Ellie had disappeared in the darkness.

He looked around the area one more time, knowing deep down that there was no time to waste so the troll squared his shoulders and headed in the direction that the red dragon had flown. It seemed, as he headed off, that there was a way to get into the Princess' world. The dragon knew it and, after all, dragons were much dumber than trolls. So whatever a dragon could do, a troll could do much better, he thought.

ABOUT THE AUTHOR

Robert is the new author of a series of books titled Witch Way Books. Robert lives in Bellingham, Washington with his wife and youngest child (along with his imaginary friend Percy, the dragon) where his second book, **Witch Way Back**, will be set. For more information you can go to witchwaybooks.com or visit him on Facebook.